Darion's Gifts

Written & Illustrated by Nina De La Mare

To Holly,

Always look for rainbows in the clouds!

Nina De La Mare

Darion's Gifts was first published, in the United Kingdom, in 2023 as an original paperback by Soul Pathways Publishing.

Ann Cottage
75 Canterbury Road
Lydden
Kent CT15 7EX
United Kingdom

Email: SoulPathwaysPublishing333@gmail.com

Copyright (c) 2023 Nina De La Mare. All rights reserved.

The rights of Nina De La Mare to be identified as the author of the artworks and text contained within these pages has been asserted by her in accordance with the Copyright, Design and Patents Act 1988

ISBN No: 978-1-7394524-0-7

In life you come across extraordinary people who guide you along the path you are meant to walk. Some call it chance, I like to think of it as synchronicity. With two Orphan wolf cubs nestled under my jumper, a spark inside me was instantly ignited.

Thank you, Tony Haighway, Founder of Wolf Watch UK, for the match that lit the flame.

To Julia James, whose encouragement and excitement spurred me on. Although you flew home before the finale, I still feel your presence gently guiding me.

To the real life characters, Lara Traub, Lawrence and Flynn Dougall, Maddie and James Warnock. Keep weaving the magic of your own stories, for they will take you where you are meant to be!

Acceptance

Wings drooping, head bowed low, Darion entered the cave and slouched down next to the fire. He scanned the earthen floor, pleading for a distraction so his tear-filled eyes wouldn't have to meet hers.

Her hot breath shot out and stoked the fire. Iridiana had felt Darion's presence, even before he had appeared. Sensing his weariness, she wondered why his heart was so full of sorrow.

"What's wrong, Darion?" his aunt asked tentatively.

"Nothing!" came the young dragon's reply.

"You have been living with me for the past two years, I know when something is on your mind."

Darion realised it was futile trying to hide the truth from her. Looking up, he stared into her mesmerising eyes. "I feel angry!" he huffed.

"Angry? What has made you feel like this?" she asked, her eyes fixed intently on her nephew.

"Today I watched the Fire Dragons learn to breathe fire. They were all so excited. It was amazing witnessing their power. Everyone was congratulating them."

"Did you not share in their joy?"

"No! I felt very envious and left out. WHY can't I breathe fire, like the other dragons?"

"Darion, you are a Water Dragon. You are talented in other ways. It is rare for a Water Dragon to be able to breathe fire."

"But not impossible! And I want to!" hissed Darion crossly, glaring bitterly at his aunt. Pain welled up inside his stomach. The only place he could direct this horrible, uncomfortable feeling was towards her. He knew it wasn't fair, but he couldn't help himself.

"Why is it important for you to breathe fire?" asked Iridiana. Her beautiful orange eyes locked gently on to his.

"I need to be a Fire Dragon! I wish to be powerful and I want to be accepted. You don't know what it is like to feel different. Everyone loves you," he grumbled. "but I am always on my own."

"Darling, I am still learning to master my power. To be accepted, you must see the magnificence inside yourself. You must recognise the true YOU. If you are unable to find within yourself that which you seek, forever you will be chasing it," whispered Iridiana.

Darion felt horrified. How dare his aunt talk to him like this? He found Iridiana could be utterly infuriating at times. He needed time to think. "It's OK for you, you know everything," he pouted, rolling his eyes. "For you, there can be nothing left to learn."

"No dragon knows everything. Every day I feel excited to learn new things," smiled his aunt.

Darion found himself leaning against the cold cave wall. He could feel the coolness seeping into his body. "Who do you learn from?" he whispered as his anger started to slip away.

With tenderness, Iridiana replied, "I learn from watching Mother Nature interact with each living creature. She is wise, never comparing one being to another. Mother Nature knows balance. Every experience I have, good or bad, teaches me. Darion, the most precious teachings have come from you."

"Me?" stammered Darion in sheer disbelief. What could HE possibly teach HER?

"Losing my sister and your father to the Malevolens made my heart icy cold. I encased the pain in a stone wall. I cared for no-one. Not even myself," whispered Iridiana sadly. "When you came to live with me, you brought music and colour to our home every day. Bit by bit, the wall started to crumble, and you helped me to remember and celebrate the happy times. You taught me to focus on being in the present moment. Darion, you are a beautiful soul. I feel blessed to have you in my life."

Darion blushed. His anger melted completely. Iridiana even noticed the beginnings of a tiny smile appearing on his face as he leaned his head against her wings.

"Will you tell me one of the stories the dragon ancestors passed down to you about the Earth People?" Darion asked, distracting her from any further conversation.

"Of course. I might even include Water Dragons in this one," she chuckled. A few bright orange sparks escaped from her flared nostrils and turned to ash. "Do you know why Water Dragons are so special?"

"Mmm... because we can breathe underwater?" replied Darion, half sarcastically.

"True," smiled his aunt, "but more importantly, the Water Dragons have the power to keep the energy of love flowing. With their smooth, snake-like bodies they are able to carry the love of the Universe wherever they go. You certainly brought universal love to me."

***

Ripples

Pulling her cardigan tightly around her, Lara gasped at the evidence of last night's storm. There were broken bits of wood everywhere, seaweed strewn across the beach. A testimony of the incredible power of nature. Sea creatures of all shapes and sizes lay helpless. Some had managed to find refuge in rock pools. Others were not so fortunate.

Crouching down on the sand, Lara began to pick up the stranded animals, releasing them into the still-unforgiving sea. She paid no attention to whether they had huge claws, googly eyes or spines covering their bodies. Even if those bodies were partially broken, she still tried to save them. Lara knew each one of these creatures needed her. In a way, she needed them too. She understood what it was like to be different, to be left out in the cold. Lara wanted to show she cared. She wanted to be a voice for those unable to speak for themselves.

The spray from the rough sea exploded around her, soaking her clothes with salty water. The garments clung to her body as the piercing wind screamed in her ears, "Leave these hapless creatures! They are not worthy! You cannot make a difference!"

Angry words raced through her mind as she knelt before the mighty ocean. Cupping her hands, Lara gently picked up a small wriggling fish and slid it back into the sea. With a flick of its tail it darted away through the waves. Lara glared at the ocean and screamed into the wind. "I made a difference to that one!"

The wind whipped furiously around her. Tears filled her eyes as she realised she would not be able to save every single creature in time. There were too many. Lara could no longer feel her fingers and toes. Her body was frozen. She staggered and almost fell, but Lara refused to give up.

Without warning, the sea ascended in an immense foaming wave. It no longer looked like a wave; it now appeared as huge, snow-capped mountains. Blinking through her tears Lara looked upwards. Towering in front of her was a giant man, sitting upon a magnificent stallion. The giant's thick white beard covered his stony face. Hair flowed behind him, trailing in the wind. In his right hand, he proudly held a silver trident above his head.

"Hold your tears!" the giant boomed. "I am Poseidon, God of the Ocean. Your tears are making the water too salty!"

Lara stared in shock at Poseidon, desperate tears still rolling down her cheeks. With quivering lips, she shouted back, straining her voice to be heard above the whirling wind, "I must help these creatures!"

"Can't you see, child? You have saved some; you cannot save them all. The ones you have saved will never forget you. Your compassion has set a great ripple in motion," Poseidon paused to let his words sink in. "You may not see the benefit of that ripple, but it has unimaginable depth and strength. In allowing your tears to flow freely, over creatures as humble as these, you have connected yourself to the sea and all that dwells within. Your power has brought me from the depths of the ocean. Come Earth Warrior, join me and I will show just how connected you are to the magic of the sea!"

Leap of Faith

Poseidon had an abrupt manner that Lara didn't really care for. What did he want with her? For a split second, she thought about disobeying him. She had read about Poseidon. Could this really be the God of the Sea? Or was she being drawn into a trap? Was it wise to defy a god? Despite her reservations, Lara grabbed hold of the strong outstretched arm, and took a leap of faith on to the back of the imposing stallion. Clinging tightly to Poseidon she no longer feared the waves as they pulled at her legs and knew with certainty she was safe.

Moving silently, the stallion morphed into the sea. Warmth oozed through her body and she realised with surprise that she could breathe beneath the waves. As her fingers began to thaw, she caressed the stallion's mane, sensing the incredible speed with which the magnificent beast moved. She had expected the sea to be dark, reflecting the mood of the clouds, but the water was light, calm and welcoming.

Under the water, orbs whirled like fireworks. A turtle glowing with bioluminescence astonished Lara as it swam gracefully past. Fish resembling parrots darted back and forth swishing their tails with glee.

Majestic stingrays crunched noisily on unsuspecting crustaceans attached to a shipwreck. Lara's jaw dropped wide open as she saw seahorses ridden by tiny people, carrying sea snails on their backs. Their hands held seaweed like bunches of flowers, and they waved to Lara as they glided past. She rubbed her eyes, struggling to believe what she was seeing.

A movement in the corner of her eye startled her, and she gasped. Drifting alongside were creatures that seemed to be a cross between mighty snakes and dragons. She could feel the snake-dragons watching her intently as they escorted Poseidon. In the background, Lara noticed colours she had never experienced before, swirling in a huge vortex. How could this be, she wondered?

As if reading her mind, Poseidon answered. "This is an underwater Kingdom. A world can exist in a single teardrop. Water is as old as the Universe and as equally majestic." Wow, thought Lara, trying to comprehend.

Poseidon continued in his bellowing voice, "Did you know the intense heat from the sun causes the water to evaporate from the ocean? It rises high up into the sky and is held in the clouds so that it may later fall and refresh Gaia. Water represents our emotions. Mother Earth is crying, right now. Have you noticed how many floods there are around the world?"

Lara shook her head. "I have never really thought about it like that before," she whispered.

"Well," huffed Poseidon, "water is always moving and changing, carving its own landscape. Like the wind, it knows freedom; it cannot be contained. Earthlings try to harness the water, to change and divert it from its true course, without concern for the consequences."

Lara thought about how people carve their own landscape. Is that what she was doing in her own life? She'd felt continually judged in her world. The weight of Lara's thoughts sometimes made it difficult for her to breathe. But here, in the sea... how lovely to be like the water and journey where life took you.

Suddenly, like life, the waters became turbulent. The snake dragons encircled Poseidon, engulfing them all in billowing sand. Lara could feel her heart pounding. Once the sand had cleared she found herself in a long cave where light shone brightly ahead. On the other side of the cave an incredible view emerged. Hundreds of ancient buildings and tumbled down rocks stretched as far as her eyes could see. In her mind Lara heard, "Welcome to Atlantis, gateway to the Lost World."

Underwater Magic

Lara barely had time to register the fact that Poseidon's words had arrived directly into her mind rather than being spoken aloud, when she realised they were not alone.

Nestled into the rocks sat merfolk. Their half-human, half fish forms thrashed silver tails in the foam. Their beautiful singing echoed throughout the city walls and into the surrounding sea like the melodic sounds of a harp.

"It's magical!" exclaimed Lara, as a multitude of sea creatures swam amongst the pillars. Bright corals shone like stage lights, and the sea floor seemed to move constantly as shoals of fish flickered, changing direction with remarkable synchronicity.

"Isn't it wonderful?" smiled Poseidon, his eyes glittering.

"An exquisite underwater world!" Lara agreed politely, thankful that she hadn't let her earlier apprehensiveness get the better of her. She sighed at the beauty of the ever-changing landscape, admiring the enormous kelp as it ebbed and flowed in rhythm with the tide. A bottlenose dolphin swam past and turned to look at her. Lara saw herself reflected in the darkness of his eyes. In that moment she had a fleeting feeling that they shared secrets from past times, but when the dolphin moved on, the feeling did too. She returned her attention to the scene before her. She had heard of the legends of Atlantis. A vast city reclaimed by water. But how could that be? As though hearing her thoughts once again, Poseidon answered.

"Now there lies a story," he teased. "Atlantis was an experiment by the Galactic Council. They love to create worlds and have created a great many!"

"You mean... there are more worlds?" she gasped.

"Of course," said Poseidon. "I have already told you that you can find a universe in a drop of water. Imagine what is possible! The Galactic Council wanted to create a place where beings could live together in peace."

"But... I thought Atlantis was built underwater," whispered Lara timidly.

"No, it wasn't always underwater. Originally Atlantis was a huge continent built on the land."

"On the Earth - how?" asked Lara in astonishment.

"The Council recruited the dragons and other beings to help construct Atlantis," replied Poseidon.

"Dragons?" Lara repeated, her mind racing.

"Yes, dragons!" bellowed Poseidon, his eyes sparkling. "There are four types. Earth, Air, Water and Fire. Each has their own role. The Earth Dragons are wise, powerful beings. They can build anything. They helped form the land, building great mountains. Earth Dragons are quite friendly to humans, you know. If you are really lucky, they may allow you to ride them."

"Wait - do you mean Earth Dragons exist now?" Lara asked, trying to concentrate but finding herself imagining how wonderful it would be to fly above the clouds.

"Of course!" replied Poseidon gruffly. "They are wisdom-keepers of the Earth's knowledge and secrets. A very responsible job. They have done this work since the dawn of time."

Lara wondered what kind of secrets the wisdom-keepers kept. She marvelled at the knowledge they must have.

"Earth Dragons come in all shapes and sizes," Poseidon continued. "Sometimes, when they leave Lemuria to visit Earth, they rest in the cumulonimbus clouds. Dragons exist on a higher frequency to humans so condensation appears around them. Occasionally you can see their outline in the clouds. They often travel at night. Why do you think you can see dark spots on the Moon?"

"Do you mean the dragons cast shadows on the Moon?" Lara asked in amazement.

"Yes!" grinned Poseidon, flashing her a knowing look.

"But... how did the Fire Dragons help create Atlantis?"

"Fire-breathing dragons created the volcanoes," said Poseidon. He seemed to be growing impatient with Lara for not knowing that which he considered obvious. "And before you ask me any more questions, Water Dragons, similar to the ones escorting us, carried enough water to fill the rivers and sea."

"Where did they collect the water from?" asked Lara.

"From comets, of course!" Poseidon replied. "Frozen balls of ice. And their cousins, the Air Dragons, took it upon themselves to guard the portal through which the comets were passed."

Lara gazed at Poseidon. A portal? It was a lot to take in. "That must have been an astonishing sight."

"It was," smiled Poseidon excitedly. "The most incredible architecture on Atlantis was the concentric circles designed to form the layout of the city. From space, these circles looked like an eye. The Galactic Council called it, 'The Eye of Horus'."

"The Eye of Horus!" beamed Lara enthusiastically, pleased to find something familiar. "It's an Egyptian symbol representing protection and healing. I have drawn it many times!"

She laughed, glancing upwards. "How incredible that must have looked from space to watch dragons guiding comets."

Pressing a finger to his lips, the King of the Sea whispered, "The circles were actually a portal to the Universe. The Galactic Council wanted to keep watch over their creation. The outer circle contained a canal that housed hundreds of great galleons!"

Lara imagined beautiful sailing ships riding the ocean waves.

After pausing for breath, Poseidon continued, "These magnificent galleons travelled the seas, trading gold and spices. Atlanteans were wealthy beyond their wildest imagination. They knew nothing of hunger or poverty. Everything they wished for could be found from the land."

Lara murmured, "Atlantis must have been a good place to live."

"You would think so, but sadly not all Atlanteans appreciated what they had," replied Poseidon. "They forgot that the ashes beneath their feet were those of their ancestors. They poisoned the land with their selfish thoughts and the poison flowed into the rivers and the sea. Their fires of destruction burnt long into the night and polluted the air. The Atlanteans forgot to teach their children that the Earth was their real mother."

"It's similar on Earth now," whispered Lara solemnly. "Many do not cherish what they have. We need to have gratitude for our planet before it is too late!"

Poseidon nodded sagely. "Your people will learn. When they fully understand the deep connection between all living things and value them equally, the destruction of your planet may be halted, and possibly reversed. They must work with Mother Nature, rather than against her. They need to learn the lessons from Atlantis."

Lara, gazed around at the amazing underwater city once more. "I do hope so..." she replied pensively.

"Come. You have yet to witness the most extraordinary sight of all!" Poseidon exclaimed, barely able to contain his excitement. He squeezed the reins, and once again the stallion sped through the aquamarine water. Everything around them blurred, and Lara felt dizzy. She felt like she was about to pass out when abruptly the mystical beast came to a halt. Beside Lara stood a colossal building that towered high up towards the surface of the ocean.

"This is my Temple. After all I am the King of the Sea!" He boasted as he puffed out his chest. "It was named after me, of course! The Galactic Council wanted to show their appreciation for all my hard work."

The Temple was taller than any building she had ever seen. Lara wondered how something so elaborate could have been constructed. Before she could ask, Poseidon again interrupted her thoughts as though he had heard what she was thinking.

"Well, you know, the Atlanteans were a very advanced race. Much more advanced than humans. They were great engineers and they moved around in small aircraft that could lift rocks with ease. It was in this Temple that the High Priests and Priestesses placed the Great Violet Crystal, after a magnificent honouring ceremony."

"The... Great Violet Crystal?"

Poseidon smiled. "Yes, a mighty crystal, powered by pure source energy. It was so strong that it energised an invisible cloak of protection over the entire land. No one could enter or leave Atlantis."

"Didn't the Atlanteans feel trapped if they couldn't leave?"

"Not at all," Poseidon boomed. "The Air Dragons made sure that the portals to the stars were kept clear, and they protected the crystal. Anyone could leave if they had a good reason. They just needed to be granted permission from the Council."

Lara gazed up at Poseidon in awe as he resumed his story, "The crystal gave free electricity to all. Atlanteans could travel all over the continent in their aircraft; however, their technical advancement eventually led to their downfall."

"What happened? gasped Lara. "How did Atlantis end up in the sea?"

"It's more a question of why," thundered Poseidon angrily. "The Atlanteans started to misuse their power. They became so attached to technology, they disengaged from who they really were. They no longer sought the solace of the land."

Lara's heart sank. It reminded her so much of what was happening back home. Poseidon continued furiously, "Many of the Atlanteans used the pure energy of the crystal to make weapons of war! Can you believe that? Fighting simply because they didn't want to share."

"History repeats itself," sighed Lara to herself.

"Neighbours fought with one another," said Poseidon, his voice tinged with sadness. "Brothers and sisters quarrelled over things of no importance. Despite warnings from the Galactic Council, Atlanteans refused to see that warring was futile."

"Why do people fight?" Lara whispered, again to herself, but this time Poseidon answered.

"There are so many reasons, Lara. It is usually to do with power or money, nothing good ever comes from war. The Galactic Council was enraged. War was not their way, for they are peaceful beings.

The Council realised that something needed to be done. Their experiment had failed."

"What did the Council do?" asked Lara

"The Galactic Council sent a violent earthquake," replied Poseidon. "A tsunami followed, causing the sea to swallow up Atlantis crashing it into the depths of the ocean. The Great Violet Crystal disappeared beneath the water."

"Oh," gasped Lara. "Was the crystal ever found?"

"Of course," snorted Poseidon. "To this day, it continues to be guarded by the Water Dragons. The crystal is important because not only is it an advanced computer, it is also an intergalactic portal. Do you know what that means?"

"Not really," replied Lara, her eyes wide open.

"It means, dear child, that one can travel to different dimensions throughout the Universe." With that, Poseidon shot his trident into the sea bed. The sand was displaced, uncovering the most amazing violet crystal. Lara could feel the energy from the crystal pulsating throughout her body.

"It's incredible!" she gasped; her eyes full of wonder. "The whole sea has changed into rainbow colours!"

"It is one of the rarest crystals in the Universe," exclaimed Poseidon proudly. "Of course, I helped the dragons bring it to Earth."

"What will happen to the crystal?" inquired Lara.

Poseidon beamed. "It will remain in the sea until one day it will be used again to create the New World, a time which will be known as the Golden Era. A world where all will live in harmony."

Lara nodded. It was all so fascinating; she wanted to know everything there was to know.

"Who do you rule over now that the Atlanteans have gone?"

"I never ruled over the Atlanteans, for they were to find their own way", replied Poseidon. "I am Guardian of the Seas, although I don't have to do much. Sea creatures abide by the Natural Law." He paused, and lowered his voice secretively. "Occasionally," he laughed, "I will ask the wind to blow a whaling ship off course. Sometimes I will help to release dolphins from fishing nets or reunite stranded seal pups with their mothers."

Lara kissed Poseidon gently on his cheek. "Thank you for showing me your world. It is magical."

Nobody had ever kissed Poseidon before. Usually anyone who met him was so terrified they either ran away, or shook so much they were unable to talk to him. He felt humbled and marvelled at the compassion this young lady had shown.

"Lara, you understand how important the world around you is. You are like a drop in the ocean. A wave cannot form without the drops coming together. I brought you here because you are an Earth Guardian. You can be the drop that helps to unite others."

"I can," she replied, her eyes shining in awe of all that she had witnessed.

"Good," muttered Poseidon. "Hold tight, it is time for me to return you to your world."

Once more Lara clung to Poseidon. The stallion moved up and down as though on a carousel, moving gently through the water. As they surfaced, Lara felt a soft breeze on her face. The wind was no longer harsh on her skin. It was almost silent. Like the storm, the wind had come and gone.

Standing on the shore, Lara noticed the sand was clear of debris. The tide must have come in and collected the marooned animals, she thought.

Lara was beginning to understand why Poseidon had told her that water was the 'Mother of the Universe', it had gathered all that belonged to her.

Poseidon bent down into the sea. As he surged out of the water, clasped in his hand was a beautiful nautilus shell. "Lara, please accept this gift from the sea. Whenever you feel alone, place the shell to your ear. You will hear the ocean's waves. Use this gift to call upon the Water Dragons if you need to. You have many allies in the ocean and they will always help if you are in need of them. You have made friends today that will forever be thankful you saved them from the storm."

Lara held the shell carefully. She loved how the light caught it, undulating over the surface and couldn't believe this beautiful gift was hers. Gazing up at the mighty Poseidon and whispered, "Thank you."

"Always remember, you are powerful," boomed Poseidon. "Allow that ripple to grow. Others will join you. When you work together like the droplets that form the wave, nothing can stop you. Each and all can make a difference!"

With those parting words, Poseidon plunged into the ocean once again, becoming at one with the sea.

Lara realised that there was so much she didn't understand. So many worlds out there she may never see. She thought about how much she had learned from a friendship that was so brief. A friendship that would have a profound effect on her.

As she danced along the shore, she understood that she had a purpose. She was an Earth Guardian. A role she would value.

Staring at the sea, Lara sang loudly, "My ripples will become waves and I WILL make a difference!"

***

Perception

Darion looked up in awe at his aunt. "Thank you for passing this story down to me. Our ancestors were very wise. How incredible it must have been for the Water Dragons to guard the crystal!"

Iridiana nodded. "The ancestors were wise. They understood the connectivity of all living things. What did you think about the gift Poseidon gave to Lara?"

"I think a nautilus shell must be an amazing shell, especially if it shimmers like the sea!" Darion yawned, suddenly feeling tired.

Iridiana made a noise of frustration. "...you think the shell is the gift?" she asked, looking deeply into Darion's eyes.

"I don't remember anything else Poseidon gave her," replied Darion sleepily.

"My darling, the gift was so much more than a shell. Maybe in your sleep, you may find the answer. Good night. Sleep well."

No answer came from Darion; he was already snoring gently!

The next morning as the sun peeked over the mountains, Darion stretched his short, stubby arms and shook his emerald wings.

He ambled over to his aunt who was cooking breakfast by the fire. "I've worked out the gift," he said with a smirk.

"Oh, you did, did you... what was it?" Iridiana teased.

"The shell is a portal, so that Lara could visit the underwater Kingdom whenever she wanted and meet with the Water Dragons."

"Wow," said Iridiana. "That's a really good way of looking at it. I hadn't thought about the gift as a portal. I like that."

"Well, what do you think the gift was then?" asked Darion, raising his eyebrows questioningly.

"I thought the gift could have meant so many different things. The gift of seeing another kingdom, and understanding there are so many different realms out there. I think Lara was lucky to have met so many mesmerising creatures. She learned she had a purpose. Her gift could be amplified, if she joined together, in harmony, with open-hearted beings."

"That's a lot of gifts," chuckled Darion. "Although I think you have missed a very important one."

"Do tell," his aunt replied, stirring pottage slowly around the cooking pot.

"I think Poseidon learned not to be so grumpy when he received the gift of friendship from Lara," grinned Darion, dipping his finger into the cast iron pot.

"Another interesting viewpoint," Iridiana smiled. "Isn't it amazing how you can hear the same story, but each listener perceives the story in their own way?

Get those sticky claws out of the pottage!" She slapped the back of his claw affectionately. "You need to get ready for dragon training."

***

Tribes

For the second time that week Darion came home from dragon training with a face like thunder. As he entered the cave he kicked a loose stone and sent it ricocheting across the floor. Plonking himself by the fire, his flared nostrils were greeted by the smell of roasted hibiscus flowers.

Darion gave his aunt 'the look', which meant: Don't ask me how my day went. She understood immediately and handed him a goblet of birch sap, in the hope that a soothing drink would ease his angry mood.

If Darion had been expecting an argument, he must have felt disappointed. His aunt had already learned patience. She simply spoke about her day, and made sure Darion was well fed. A hungry dragon is always a grumpy one, she chuckled to herself.

Nestled by the warmth of the fire, Darion gave his aunt a sideways glance, checking to see if she was watching him. She was.

"Aunty," he muttered. "Why am I so different?"

"Different? What do you mean?"

"Your scales are the colours of the rainbow," Darion replied, in a voice tinged with sadness. "Mine are grey, and so very dull."

"Darion, my scales are not really rainbow colours," smiled Iridiana.

"Of course they are!" he replied, furiously. "I can SEE them, shining brightly. You have the most colourful scales in all Lemuria! All the other dragons admire you for it!"

"They are bright," his aunt replied, "but they became brighter when I found joy in my life. The brightness you see is me radiating that happiness."

"What brings you joy?" Darion whispered.

"Seeing the sun rise. Feeling the earth under my feet and having your claws clasped in mine," came her thoughtful reply.

As ever, Darion found himself wanting to open up to his aunt and tell her the source of his displeasure. "This morning," he said, crossly. "The Air Dragons laughed at me for my dull scales. They said I can vanish into the landscape and no one would be able to see me."

"It's true. Nobody would be able to see you." Iridiana replied.

"I don't understand," said Darion, in sudden anger. "How can you agree with them?"

"Let me finish," replied his aunt gently. "Darion, you are a Water Dragon. You can shapeshift, and decide where you want to spend your time. It's incredible how seamlessly you blend into the environment. That is your skill and your gift."

"But I don't care about blending in," insisted Darion. "I want colourful scales, like you!"

"Your smooth scales were created to glide through the water. Without these subtle tones you would not be able to merge in with the oceans, or be able to ride the clouds without being seen by the humans."

"But why don't I want to be seen?" he cried. "Am I really that ugly?"

"Darion. You are putting your thoughts into my words. Please listen to what is ACTUALLY being said," his aunt admonished firmly. "You would frighten the humans because of your size, not because of how you look. If the Earthlings could see you, you would not be able to help them, which is your Lemurian life purpose. Humans are not ready to see you just yet! Your disguise means you can visit beautiful landscapes and not be noticed. It's like a cloak of invisibility! How fantastic is that?"

"But I want to shine brightly so that I can make friends easily," Darion hissed.

"When you make friends, it is not how you look on the outside, but rather what comes from within," replied his aunt, stroking his wings gently.

"I don't understand," huffed Darion, shaking his head sadly.

"We are all born looking different on the outside. We have different scales and come in a range of shapes and sizes. But inside our bodies, we are the same. We share the same blood. It courses through our veins and our hearts," Iridiana sighed. "What makes us different is our thoughts and how we interact with the world around us. Do we grow from the challenges we face or do hide and let fear steal our dreams?"

She continued with a faraway look in her eyes. "Our uniqueness makes us what we are. We dragons are both strong and weak. There are special types of dragons and they are often misunderstood. These dragons like being alone. They are free spirited and think deeply; they have a connection to the Universe that burns within their soul. Often they will fly and walk through the most painful lives but they have the courage to smile and help others. Dragons like these are gifts from the Universe.

"Was my mother a gift from the Universe?"

"Yes, your mother was a very special dragon. She was like the hummingbird who discerns which flowers to drink nectar from. She would help anyone, yet she chose her friends carefully. True friends are like the stars in the sky. They shine light in the darkest places and although you can't always see them, a silver thread connects you. True friends know your flaws but love you just the same."

"I think differently from lots of dragons too," cried Darion.

"And this is what truly makes you unique...your soul."

"What's a soul?" he asked.

"Your soul is the essence of who you are. It is your emotions, your inspirations, your consciousness," Iridiana replied. "When we align with dragons that match our vibration, they become true friends. Souls can recognise like-minded spirits, and these souls become our tribe."

"Are the Water Dragons my tribe?"

"Not necessarily, Darion. Your tribe will be dragons that you can relate to. Dragons who share similar ideas and like similar things. Dragons who love you for who YOU are. Listen carefully to your soul's whispers."

"Are your scales bright because your soul shines through?" whispered Darion in sudden realisation.

"Yes," Iridiana nodded. "And yours will shine brightly too, when you learn to welcome love and not anger into your life."

Darion did hold anger in his heart. He just wasn't sure yet how to let go. He could feel his rage gnawing away at him. Sometimes it consumed him and took him to a place inside himself that scared him. A place he desperately wanted to escape from. Resting his chin on Iridiana's shoulder he asked her to tell him another ancestral story.

"Come and warm yourself by the fire and I will see what springs to mind," Iridiana smiled.

Darion felt the softness of his aunt as he knelt down beside her. He could sense the gentle beating of her heart and feel the warmth from her body. He liked the comfortable feeling it gave him. It made him feel safe.

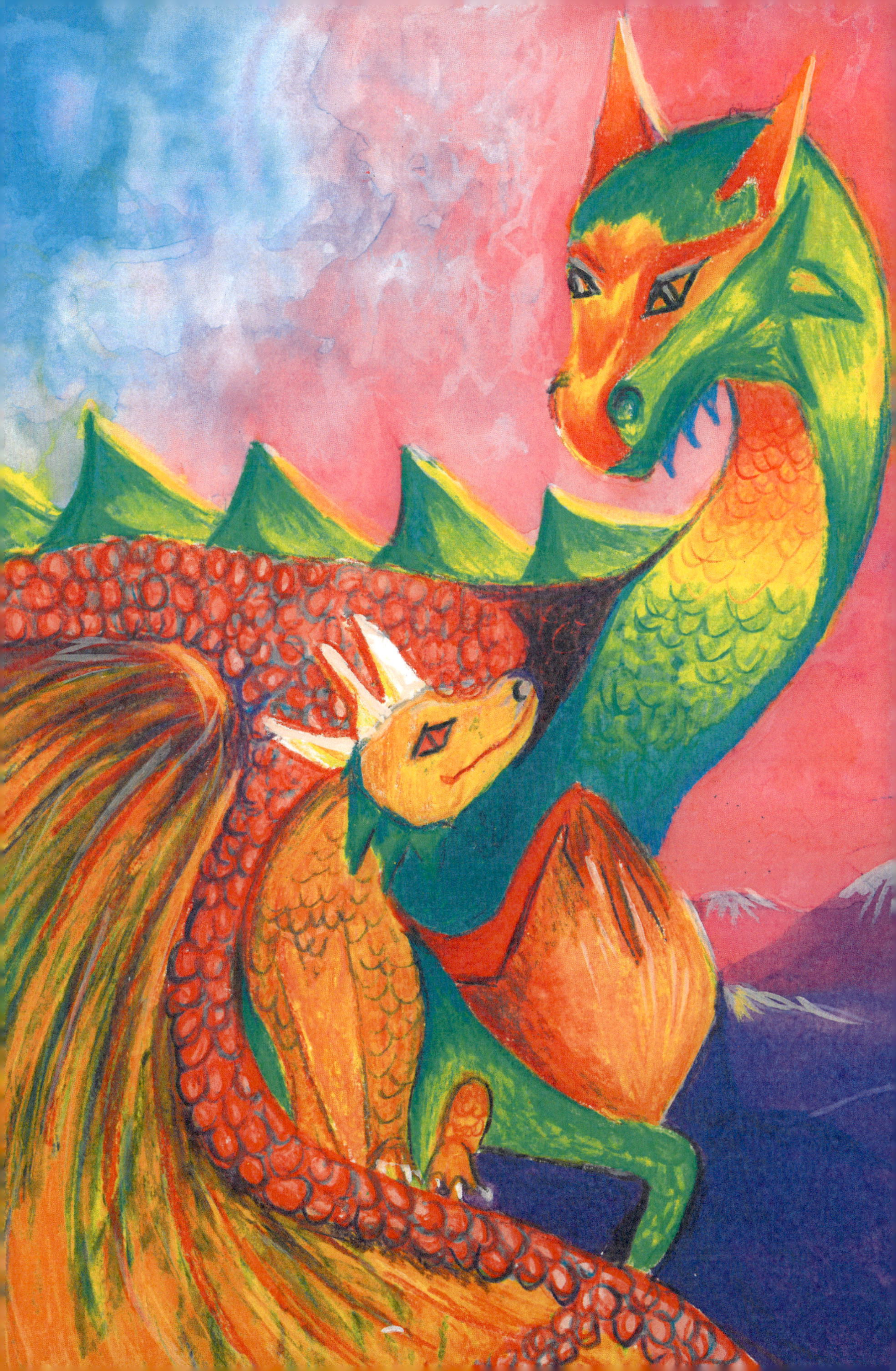

Powerful Thoughts

Lawrence had wanted to visit Grandpa for a very long time, and at last the day had finally come. It was almost two years since he had last visited, but Lawrence could still remember Grandpa Lupus' small stone cottage, encircled by giant redwood trees. Trees so tall, he thought, they must surely be able to touch the starlit sky.

"Have you packed everything you need?" Lawrence's mother called upstairs.

Lawrence puffed as he struggled with the zipper on his backpack. "I think so," he replied, clipping his penknife and torch to a loop on the zip. Checking his pockets, he felt for his asthma pump and the lucky coin his father had given him. He grabbed Chinook's threadbare collar and slipped it gently over the excited dog's neck. As he thudded downstairs with Chinook close at his heels, Lawrence's mother looked at him with exasperation.

"You are not taking Chinook with you. Your Grandpa has far too many dogs to look after as it is!"

Lawrence thought about arguing with his mother but knew it would be futile. Feeling a pang of guilt, he reluctantly removed Chinook's collar. His fluffy friend wagged his tail frantically whilst looking at him with pleading eyes. I know, thought Lawrence, reading Chinook's mind... maybe staying with Grandpa Lupus wasn't going to be much fun after all.

Grandpa Lupus lived many miles away. Maybe this was why the visits were so infrequent. Lawrence knew that it was a struggle for his mother to find enough money for the petrol. She had been so full of anger over the last couple of years.

Was she angry at him, or was it because Dad had left them just before Christmas? Lawrence could sense how apprehensive his mother was about him spending time away from her. In fact, this would be his first time. Maybe this was why she looked so sad.

After what seemed like hours the car turned off the main road and onto a disused track. Towering trees huddled over the pathway, with huge branches that met in the middle as though shaking hands with each other. The light above dimmed as the harvest-coloured sun's rays cascaded behind the trees. It felt like a place time stood still. It was so tranquil. Trees seemed to whisper secrets from centuries past to each other. Lawrence felt the hairs on his neck stand up as the car rattled deeper into the woods.

As the car came to an abrupt halt, excitement welled up inside Lawrence. He grasped the door handle. Thrusting the door open, he stumbled out on to a bank of dew-covered moss. Grandpa Lupus stood before him. He was not quite as tall as Lawrence remembered, but other than that, he looked exactly the same. He still had a mass of grey hair and tortoiseshell-rimmed glasses that hung from the end of his wrinkled nose.

"You have grown so much!" exclaimed Grandpa.

Lawrence smiled at his Grandpa and gave him a hug breathing in the familiar smell of beeswax furniture polish. Grandpa was an amazing carpenter. Lawrence fondly remembered the beautiful spinners he used to make for him.

"Take your bag, then," said Lawrence's mother, handing him his backpack. She enfolded him in another hug and whispered in his ear, "I have to go now before it gets too dark. I shall pick you up in a few days.

Make sure you are polite and helpful; your grandfather needs looking after. You are staying in the most amazing place. Remember to listen to the silence. It's only in the silence that you truly hear."

She kissed the top of his head and without looking back, his mother climbed into the car and drove away. Lawrence felt deserted. He knew Grandpa was a kind man, but he hadn't seen him for a couple of years and he wondered if they would still have fun together.

Inside the stone wall cottage was an open fire. Large pine logs blazed with warmth. The smell of roasted chestnuts reminded Lawrence how empty his stomach felt. It seemed like hours since he had last eaten. Peering around, he noticed an assortment of leather-bound books, crammed into a rather unusual bookcase. The red grain of the shelves gleamed with light from the flickering flames. It was almost as if the books were watching him. Imagine all those ideas and information; why, Grandpa must know everything!

Cobwebs of silver thread draped the books like silk scarves. Lawrence marvelled at the detail in the webs and the delicateness of nature. How could something so delicate be so strong? Sometimes, pondered Lawrence, people can be like that too.

Grandpa Lupus noticed Lawrence looking at the shelves in awe.

He told Lawrence that the wood had come from an ancient yew tree, just the other side of the lake. "The yew is a very special tree. It can live for many centuries. It is the tree of magic, from which the most marvellous wands can be crafted," chuckled Grandpa Lupus, with a twinkle in his eye.

"That's incredible," grinned Lawrence. "Did you make these shelves, Grandpa?"

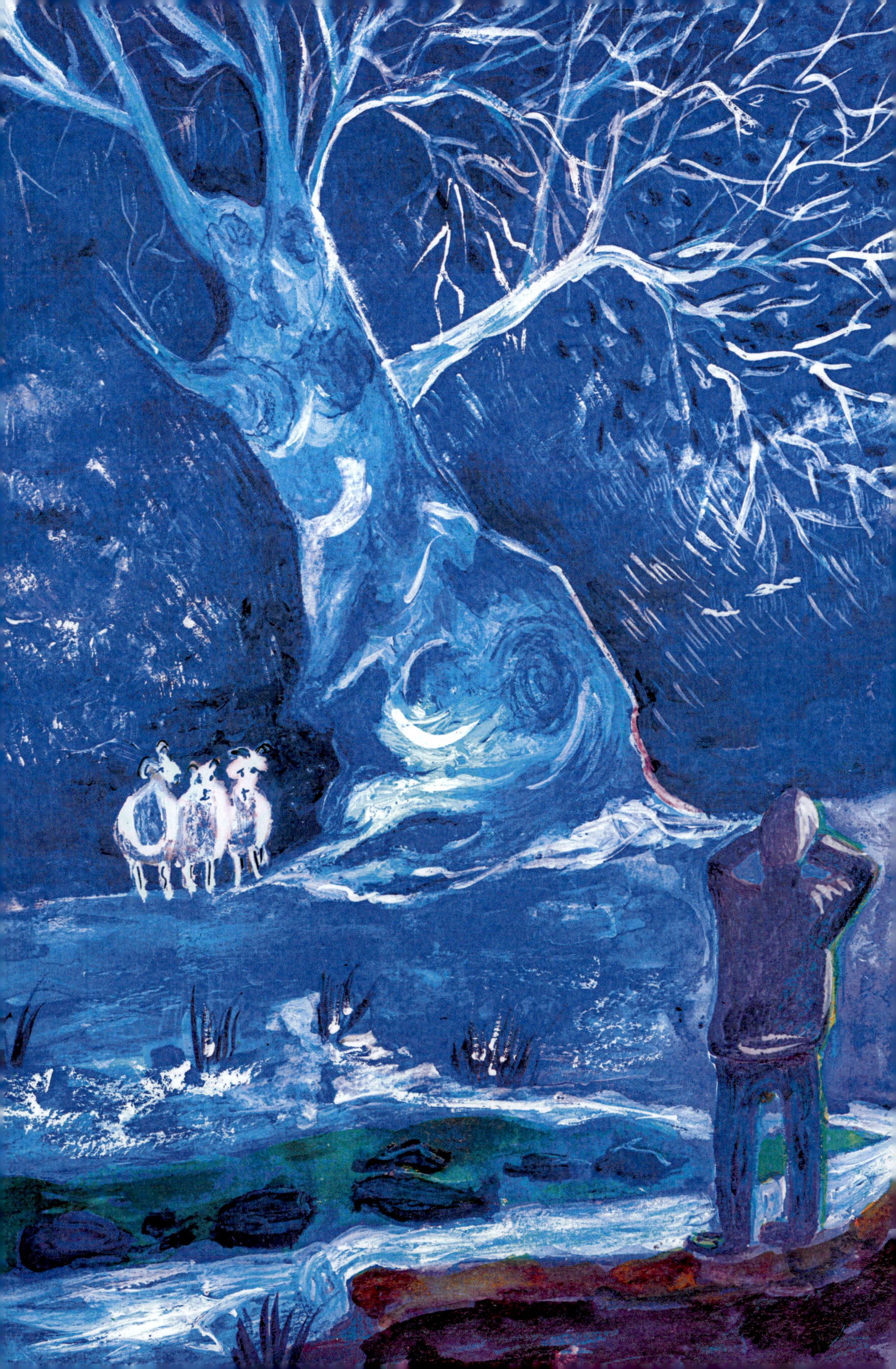

Grandpa thought for a while before he answered. "Aye, I did, lad, from a fallen yew tree. One stormy winter evening, when I was checking the sheep, the sky lit up with a violet haze. A bolt of lightning shot right through the middle of the yew tree like a ball of fire. The tree fell heavily onto the ground."

"Ohhh," said Lawrence, his blue eyes widening as he tried to imagine the scene. "You saw it happen?"

Grandpa cleared his throat. "I was looking for my naughty sheep dog, Sirocco. As I approached the yew, lightning struck the tree."

"What did you do, Grandpa?"

"The yew seemed to fall in slow motion, but I still couldn't move fast enough. Down it came... just caught my leg as I turned to run away. I was trapped! The wind was driving icy droplets of rain into my face, and they stung. I was so shocked. I closed my eyes. I had given up hope," said Grandpa as he gazed into the open fire.

Lawrence whispered, "But you are still here, Grandpa. What happened?"

Grandpa shrugged. "I am not sure. I passed out, and when I woke up... it must have been several hours later. The sun was just poking over the treetops. I could feel the warmth on my cheeks," he smiled. "The forest seemed alive with rustling noises and the magnificent cry of the buzzards flying overhead and the wonderful sound of wolves howling. The tree was beside me, but my leg was no longer trapped. Perhaps the rain had turned the ground muddy, and in my sleep, my leg may have slipped free. I looked up at the sky and was so very thankful. I remember being told as a child, that after a storm the sun always comes out. How true that is."

"Grandpa, you were very lucky!" exclaimed Lawrence.

"Yes, I know," chuckled Grandpa. "Alas, my leg was never the same after the accident. It slowed me down for sure but I never let that stop me doing anything. I couldn't let that splendid tree go to waste nor my adventure be forgotten. I made bookshelves and a walking stick out of the yew. I have all the time in the world to read now. Sometimes, I think things happen to slow us down, so we can go within and find parts of us that are lost."

Lawrence loved Grandpa's story and wanted to listen to more. But day had turned to night. It was time for bed. He yawned and rubbed his eyes. "Goodnight Grandpa."

Grandpa ruffled Lawrence's blond hair. "Goodnight lad," he said fondly.

In bed, Lawrence gazed at the stars and the Moon shining brightly through the bedroom window. The bird songs had ceased apart from the owl hooting in the woods, and the occasional fox barking. Within minutes he was sleeping peacefully.

In the early hours of the morning Lawrence woke suddenly from a deep sleep. In the coolness of the night air, he could hear howling echoing around his room. A strange feeling spread from the top of his head. It was like a shiver. He could feel the presence of something in his room. Lawrence pulled the old moth-eaten army blanket around himself tighter. I'm just having a dream, he told himself. The clouds are frolicking in the moonlit sky, forming shadows above my bed, he thought as he dozed back to sleep.

Feeling warmth on his face, Lawrence became aware of the early morning sun peering through the window, filling the room with autumn colours. The birds shook their glorious feathers and burst into a chorus of song.

He clambered out of bed and ambled into the kitchen where the smell of a cooked breakfast greeted him. The warmth in Grandpa Lupus' smile made Lawrence feel at home.

"Did you sleep well, young man?" Grandpa asked as he set Lawrence's breakfast on the table.

"I think so," replied Lawrence as he pulled out a chair and sat down. "Although I did hear strange noises."

"What sort of strange noises?" puzzled Grandpa, looking rather confused.

Lawrence speared a mushroom with his fork and looked up. "Well, I think your dogs must have been outside howling at the Moon, Grandpa."

"Zephyr and Sirocco were in my room last night. They weren't howling, they were snoring," replied Grandpa.

"But Grandpa..." Lawrence frowned, "I definitely heard howling!"

"Perhaps you have inherited the special gift," smiled Grandpa.

"Gift? What gift?"

"The gift of Canis lupus."

"I don't understand. What is Canis lupus?" asked Lawrence.

Smiling proudly, Grandpa replied, "Canis lupus are wolves. These ancient forests were once alive with wolves. They roamed freely in peace with our ancestors, who only used the resources they needed. There were no locks on doors. If something was needed, it was given. This could be a warm fur skin, a smile, or simply someone to sit with." Grandpa lent towards Lawrence and looked at him solemnly.

"It is said that only a person who is truly in harmony with nature will feel the spirit of the wolves."

Lawrence thought for a moment. "Why are wolves only here in spirit if we lived in peace with them?"

"Once, our ancestors belonged to the sacred circle of nature. All lives held equal value. Sadly, times have changed. People used the land for other things. They stepped out of the circle, no longer wanting to share with each other. More and more was taken from the land but not replaced. Things that once held value were put aside. Our ancestors turned their back on the natural laws. Wolves are one of many animals that have disappeared over the last few centuries."

Lawrence was puzzled. "But why did I hear the wolves, Grandpa?" he asked.

Grandpa scratched his chin thoughtfully. "Perhaps they are trying to tell you something. Perhaps they want you to learn about the way to be. Our ancestors lived and hunted with them in this forest. Maybe the wolves wanted you to experience what it was like to hear their amazing howl."

Gazing at the old man in wonder, Lawrence whispered, "Have you got the special gift, Grandpa?"

"After my accident I often thought I heard wolves. It's a call that I will remember all my life, but I have never seen them," he said wistfully. "Your beautiful grandmother was clear sighted. She often saw them! Oh, how I would have loved that gift. But we are all different, we all have different gifts."

Breakfast was finished in thoughtful silence. Abruptly, Lawrence stood up. "Grandpa, it's such a beautiful day! Can we try and find the wolves?"

Grandpa laughed, "Young man, my legs are old, my eyesight weak. You will only find the wolves if they want to be found. They are shy spirits. There is, however, nothing to stop you looking!" He wagged his wrinkled finger at Lawrence, "Make sure you stick to the paths. I don't want to come looking for you at teatime!"

"You don't need to worry about me Grandpa, my lungs are so bad I won't get far."

"Lawrence, be mindful of your thoughts. Thoughts are very powerful."

"I don't understand what you mean," replied Lawrence.

"If you tell yourself something enough times, you will believe it, whether that something is good or bad. Always be conscious of your thoughts, and make sure you use them in a positive way. Your body hears you!"

Lawrence wasn't sure what Grandpa meant but felt a surge of excitement as he waved goodbye. He ambled happily along the gravel path. The further away from the stone cottage he walked, the darker the forest grew. The sun was blocked by overhanging fingers of trees and the path crumbled away until it was no more.

Lawrence wondered whether he should go any further. He emptied his trouser pockets. There must be something in here that will help me decide. He found an empty chocolate wrapper, a piece of string, wrinkled conker and his lucky coin.

Clasping the coin tightly in his hand, tails I go on, heads I turn back. As he tossed the coin he could feel the anticipation welling up inside him. The coin landed softly on a carpet of bright green moss.

"Tails" shrieked Lawrence with delight. "I shall follow the direction of the sun!"

He walked for almost a mile before stopping to listen to the breeze. It reminded him of what his mother said to him: "Only in the silence do you truly hear". He was now beginning to understand not only what she meant but also what his Grandpa meant by the power of thought.

His fascination grew as a line of wood ants marched across a rotting log, carrying small leaves and twigs. He marvelled at the cooperation between the ants, and speculated on whether they ever fought with one another.

He was desperate to hear the sounds of the wolves again. Suddenly, a fox shot past him. Then a young stag. Lawrence frowned. How odd. Next came some squirrels, followed by a tawny owl whizzing by. Fear paralysed him as he realised he could smell burning.

Once again his mum's words came back to guide him. "When you feel frightened it is important to face your fear. Stand up tall, look it straight in the eye. Fear is contained in the mind. Acknowledge and thank the fear for what it has taught you, then send it on its way. Fear is the thief of all dreams!"

With those thoughts he started to run in the same direction as the animals - he didn't want to face a fire; he wasn't strong enough. The moments he had spent standing still could cost him dearly. The fire was gaining on him quickly, the smoke and fear was affecting his asthma. Without warning he stumbled on a rock. His chest felt heavy with the effort of breathing. Through his tears he noticed the ants instinctively change direction moving away from the fire.

Lawrence sobbed. One of his legs was bleeding heavily. He watched the blood trickle down, staining his sock. He was in too much pain to move. "Help! Please help me!" he shouted, as the fire sped towards him.

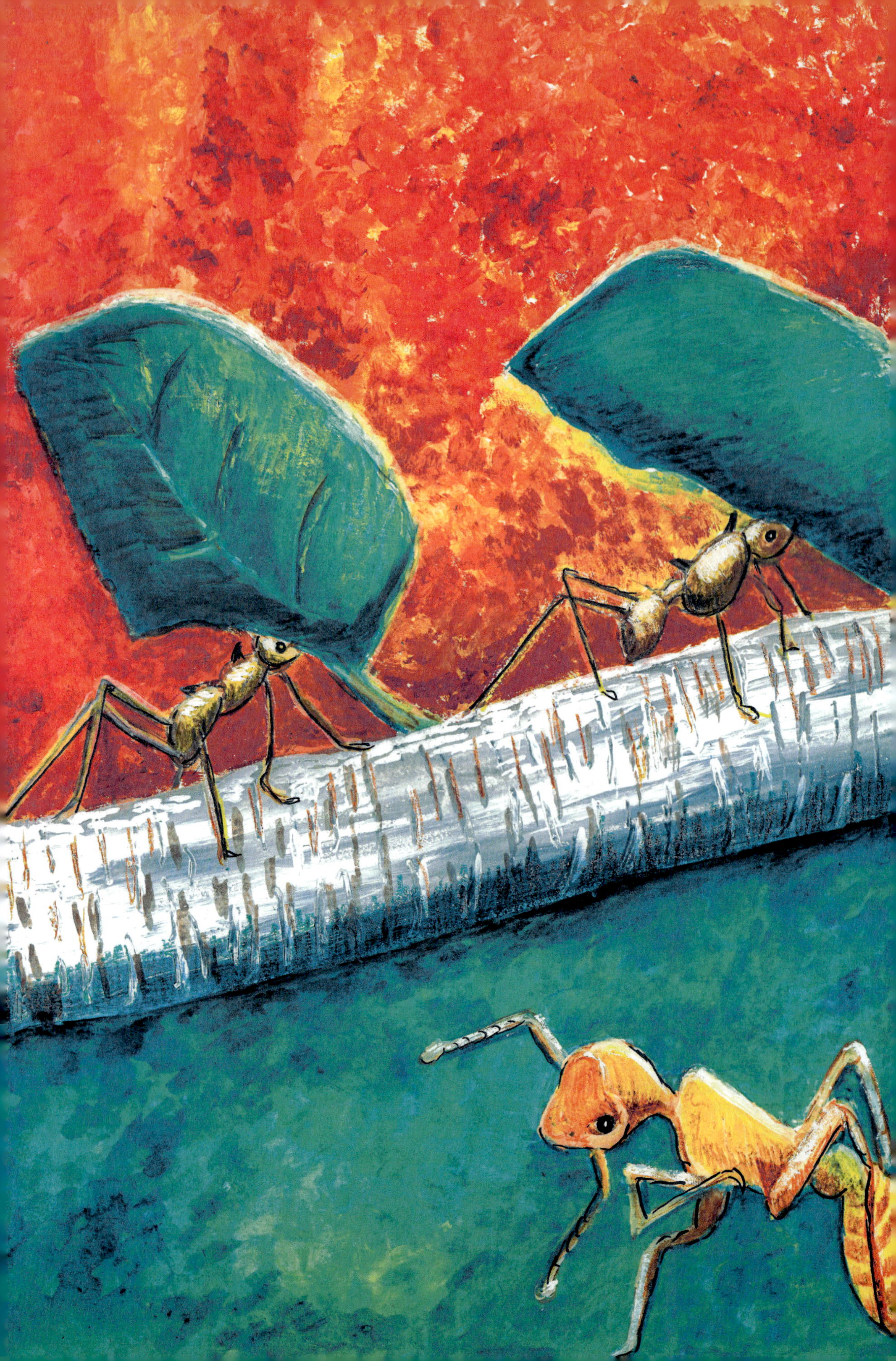

The pine needles on the forest floor were tinder-dry, perfect for feeding the flames. The crackle and roar was deafening and filled Lawrence with terror. In his mind he could hear Grandpa Lupus saying "Thoughts are powerful, be careful how you use them."

Desperately, Lawrence closed his eyes and imagined it raining and the rain extinguishing the fire. It's working, he thought excitedly, then realised it was just his own tears still flowing. He told his mind to concentrate. Slowing his breathing down, he imagined his Grandpa coming to find him.

Lawrence felt the presence of something large by his side. The hairs on his arms stood on end. Through his tears, he saw the most wondrous sight he had ever seen. A pack of seven wolves with glorious fur stood before him. Their eyes reflected the approaching fire and shone like amber in the surrounding darkness. He shivered as he noticed their glistening white teeth. Intuition told him that they were not there to harm him.

The largest wolf spoke, "Don't feel afraid. I am Nanook. We heard your cries and have come to help you escape the burning forest." Nanook gently placed his mouth around Lawrence's grubby jumper and swung him onto his back.

Lawrence felt his hands sink into the soft, thick comforting fur of Nanook. The wolves sped through the blazing forest like the wind, as flames danced by their feet. Soon the fire receded and the black pungent smoke vanished as quickly as it had appeared. Lawrence breathed more easily.

The remaining journey was smooth. The wolves' paws seemed to hover and glide over the evergreen floor. He wondered if he might be dreaming. Instinct told him he wasn't. The wolves slowed to a halt. Nanook set Lawrence down on the cold stony ground.

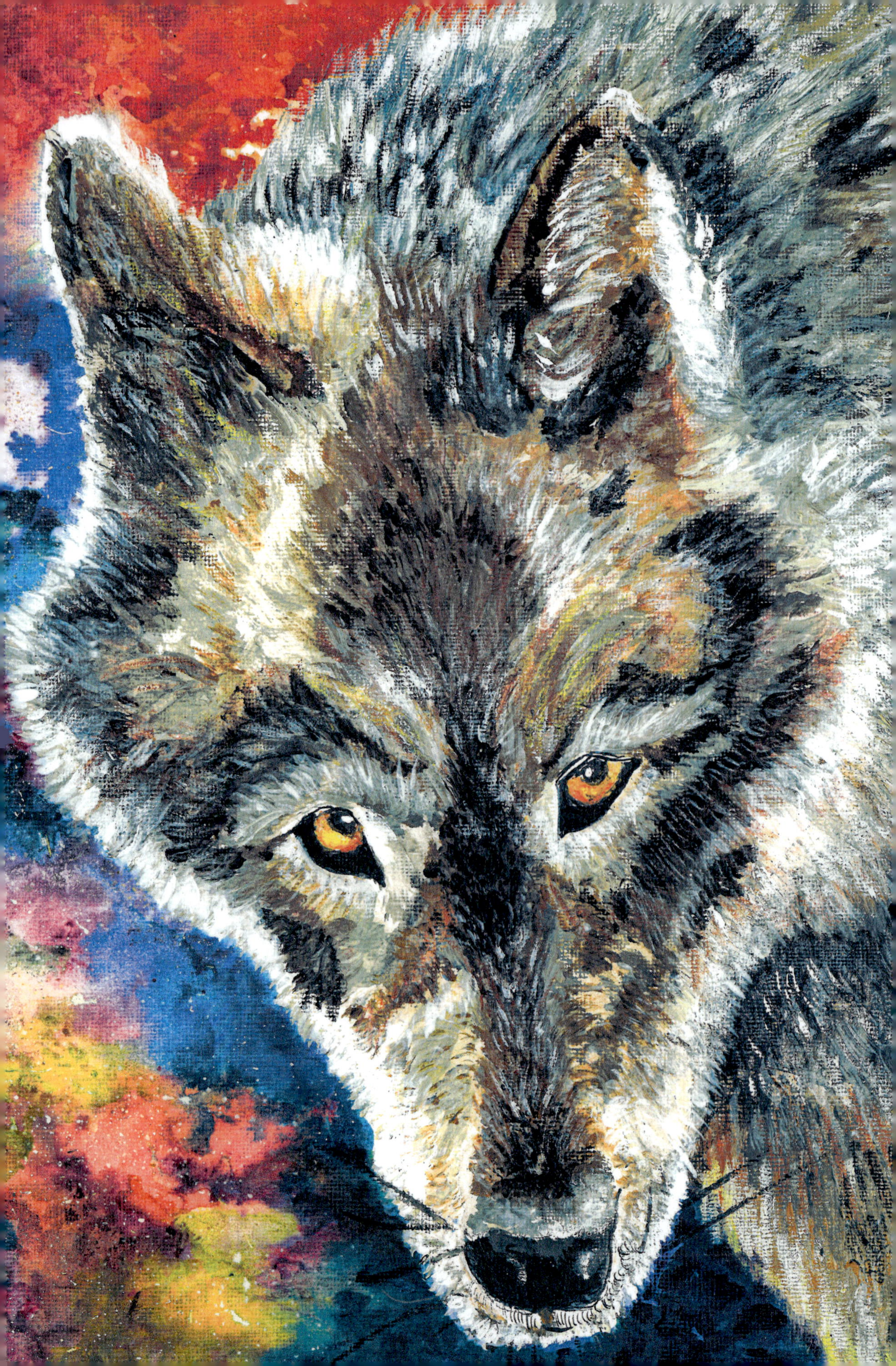

This was such a contrast after the comforting silver fur Lawrence had been grasping. "Where am I?" he asked.

Nanook replied, "You are by our den, safe away from the fire."

Becoming aware of the pain in his leg, Lawrence looked down. His leg was caked in dry blood and mud. A smaller wolf approached him and began to lick it tenderly. "What are you doing?" gasped Lawrence, wriggling and laughing as the wolf's ticklish tongue gently reached out over his leg.

"Keep still!" chuckled the small wolf. "I can help your leg heal by licking it."

With tears in his eyes, Lawrence whispered to Nanook, "Is my grandpa safe?"

Nanook lifted his heavy matted paw and placed it on Lawrence's shoulder. "Do not worry, the wind did not blow the fire in your grandpa's direction. He is on his way to find you, with the help of others."

Puzzled, Lawrence asked, "How do you know?"

"I know your Grandpa's scent. I met him long ago. We are omnipresent and have vision beyond that of our eyes. Our ears can hear the voices of other worlds. We know the scent and smell of every creature that has ever passed through this land, from the beginning of time to this very day."

Thinking about all the animals who had not been as lucky as he had, Lawrence asked how the fire had started.

"Sometimes fires are started by natural events like lightning. These can be beneficial to the plants and animals. When the fire has gone, new life will begin to appear. The old burnt trees will decay in the soil, giving a helping hand to young trees.

The circle of life continues." Nanook hung his head sadly. "This fire was started by a campfire that had not been put out properly. Many of our animal friends have lost their homes and will go hungry through this carelessness."

Lawrence put his arms around Nanook's neck. "Have you lost your home?"

"We lost our home centuries ago. Now we wander through the forests of the world, watching over future generations of wolves. I suppose you could say that we are the guardians of the forest."

"The other night, was it your pack who howled, and came into my room?"

Nanook licked some of the mud and tear stains from Lawrence's face. "Yes. You are a child of nature. We wanted you to experience the call of wild wolves." Nanook sniffed the air intently. "We must leave you now, for your grandpa is nearby."

Lawrence hugged Nanook. "Thank you for saving my life. Will I ever see you again?"

"Perhaps," replied Nanook softly, "Members of our family are always with you."

"How?" Lawrence asked, confused.

"You have a four-legged friend named Chinook, do you not? He and every dog in the world is part of our family. You will never be alone. Goodbye, my friend. Remember all that you have experienced today."

Nanook turned and led the pack away. As the wolves vanished, Lawrence felt a part of himself disappear with them.

Lawrence could hear a car approaching. A Land Rover parked by the rocks. The doors opened and Lawrence could just make out the figure of Grandpa with his walking stick, accompanied by two strangers. Lawrence waved frantically with his arms.

"Is that you, Lawrence?" bellowed Grandpa.

"Yes! I am OK, but I have hurt my leg!"

Lawrence could see people clambering up over the rocks with a stretcher. After a few minutes a Forest Ranger knelt next to him. "Hello, Lawrence. My name is Ben. Your grandpa was sure that you would be out this far. He encouraged us to search for you here. It is remarkable that you have managed to run such a distance… especially with an injured leg."

"Nanook and his family rescued me," explained Lawrence. He glanced up at his Grandpa, who had a knowing twinkle in his eye. The Forest Ranger removed his hat and scratched his head.

"Nanook? That's an unusual name. Who is Nanook, and where is he now?"

"He is a magnificent wolf. He carried me on his back. Nanook and his family travel through the forests of the world keeping watch. Grandpa, they knew you were coming!" exclaimed Lawrence, with the biggest grin ever.

Ben said nothing for a few seconds, then raised an eyebrow. "Your grandson, Mr Lupus, seems to be suffering from shock. Not uncommon after a traumatic event like this. May I suggest you get him checked over by a doctor as soon as possible."

Later that evening humming happily, Grandpa roasted chestnuts over the open fire. Lawrence eyed him sleepily. "Grandpa, how did you know where I was?"

With a sideways glance, Grandpa smiled and looked up at a beautiful oil painting of a huge silver wolf and his family, sitting on an enormous pile of rocks.

"Your Grandma knew how much I wanted to see a wolf, so she painted what she saw in her mind, a group of seven wolves on the rocks. That way I could enjoy seeing the wolves too. When the fire came, my attention kept getting drawn to your Grandma's painting. I had this inexplicable feeling that you were safe on those rocks.

Lawrence was silent for a few minutes. "Grandpa, why didn't the ranger believe me?"

"Many people need to see to believe. Your grandma would always say that you needed to believe to see. The wolves are invisible to most people. You have been blessed. Only a true child of nature inherits the gift of Canis lupus."

***

"Well," smiled Darion, "It's easy to work out what the 'gift' in this story was."

"What do you think the gift was?" laughed Iridiana.

"Being in nature, of course," winked Darion, with a cheeky grin. "What do you think it was?"

"I think the gift was Lawrence meeting his grandfather after such a long while," replied his aunt. "Maybe now Lawrence understands the power of his own thoughts?"

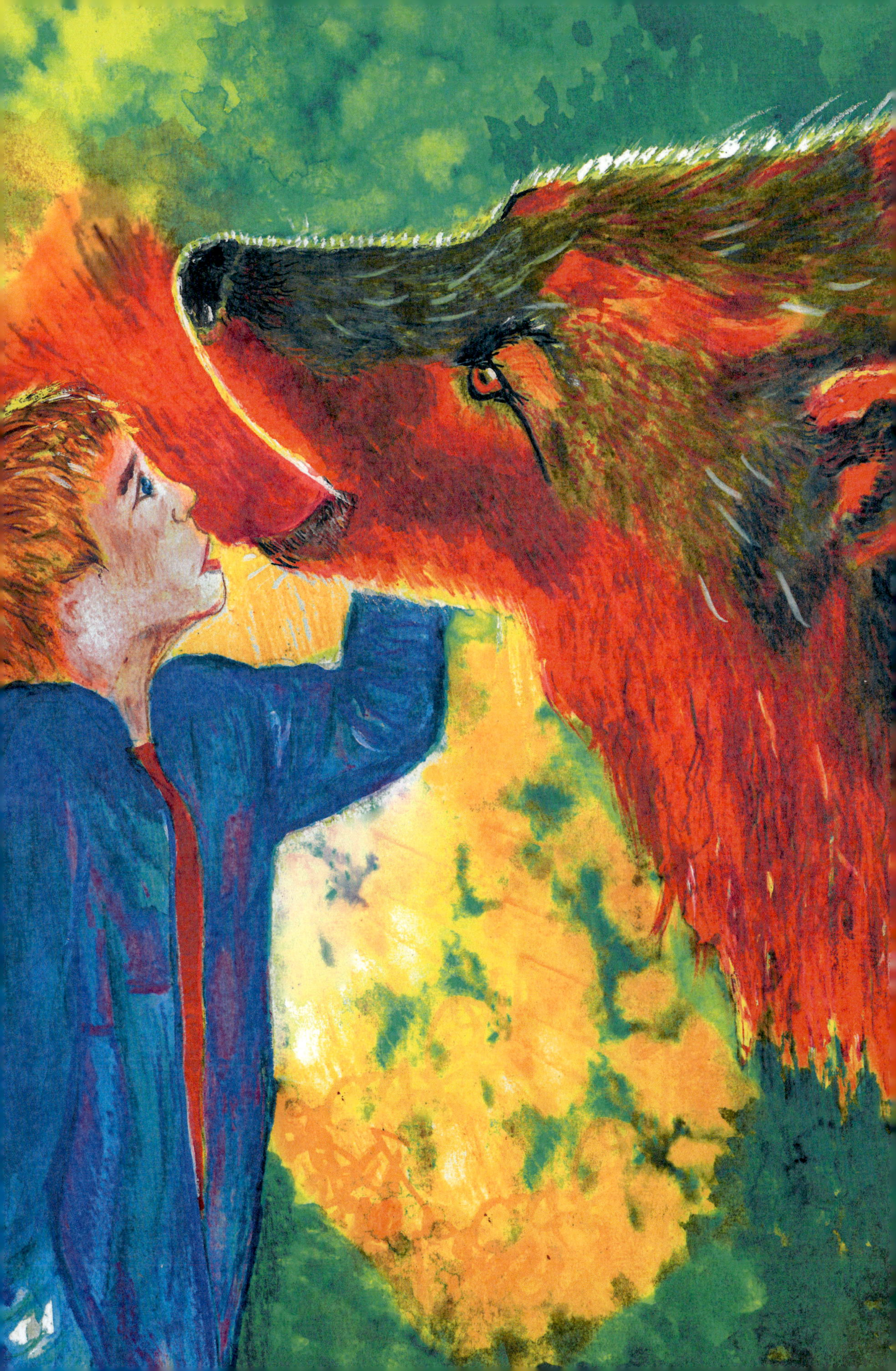

Standing In Your Power

Iridiana tapped her claws impatiently on the ground. Darion should have been home by now. A few days had passed since she told him the story of Lawrence and the wolves, and he seemed to have been dealing with his anger much better. Now, his non-appearance was worrying her. What could possibly be keeping him? It's not like him to be late, she thought. With that, she decided to look for him.

Iridiana unfolded her magnificent wings and took off majestically. She tried not to bring too much attention to herself, but her radiance brought approving looks from the dragons far below. She really was the most colourful dragon in the Kingdom of Lemuria.

As Iridiana scanned the landscape from the skies, she spotted Darion easily. His angry mood stood out a mile! He was standing by the ocean, forcefully skimming stones across the water.

"Darion, is everything OK?" she asked as she landed next to him. "I was expecting you home for supper."

For several seconds there was silence. Turning slowly, he looked up at his aunt. A single tear rolled down his cheek. "I feel so ashamed," he sobbed.

"Why do you feel like this? frowned his aunt.

"It's not what I did, it's what I didn't do," replied Darion with a trembling lip.

"Would you like to tell me about it?" Iridiana asked gently.

"No... you will be ashamed of me too."

"Darion, there is nothing you can do to stop me loving you."

'Perhaps if you tell me what happened you might feel better?"

Darion looked into his aunt's comforting eyes and nodded. He felt dreadful, but maybe talking about it might help. "The Earth Dragons were being very mean to the new dragon, Skywing. They said all sorts of horrible things to him and made him really sad. I am wondering if he will even be able to face dragon training tomorrow."

"Did you join in too?" Iridiana asked, looking directly into his eyes.

"No, I didn't say a word," replied Darion hastily.

"Then why the tears? You have nothing to be sorry about. You didn't join in."

"That's just it. I didn't say a word. I just watched. I let them be unkind," muttered Darion tearfully. "What kind of a dragon does that make me?"

"Ahh... now I understand what is troubling you," replied Iridiana. "Why did you feel unable to say anything to stop the Earth Dragons' unkind words?"

"I was shocked at their behaviour but I didn't want the Earth Dragons to be hurtful to me as well." Darion seemed to choke on his words. "So I let them carry on with their cruelty."

"Darion, I am glad you have had the courage to tell me what happened. You understand the part you played. You took responsibility for your actions" smiled Iridiana. "What you have learned today will make tomorrow better."

Darion was confused. "How will tomorrow be better? How can I face Skywing ever again?"

"Tell me," said Iridiana. "What will you do tomorrow, if the Earth Dragons are cruel to anyone else?"

"I will speak up," replied Darion solemnly.

"Good, then you have learned how to respond to those that bully others. Tomorrow you will stand in your own power," said Iridiana, looking directly into her nephew's eyes.

"My own power? What do you mean?"

"Standing in your power is about reaching down into the depths of yourself to find your true voice and inner strength. You speak YOUR truth even if others are not ready to hear what you say. Embracing the concept that everything in life happens for a reason. Nobody can take your power away from you, unless YOU let them. It's simply about knowing oneself."

Darion absorbed her words quietly. "Why do some dragons take pleasure in being unkind?" he whispered, feeling very small indeed.

Iridiana shuffled close to her nephew and draped a comforting wing around him. "Sometimes it makes them feel in control, but underneath they are probably feeling sad and scared. Dragons who are unkind have usually been treated badly themselves, and they act out their pain on others as a way of feeling in control. It takes a brave dragon, one that stands in their own power, to break the cycle. Darion, you realised your mistake yourself and how to resolve it. You didn't need me at all."

Darion shook out his wings and stood up straight. Iridiana felt he was growing taller before her eyes. Wiping his mucky face with his claws, Darion asked if his aunt could tell him a story about the earth-bound mortals.

"Mmm... I suppose so, but it's straight home afterwards otherwise your favourite broth will have boiled dry," she chuckled as they sat down on the soft sand.

***

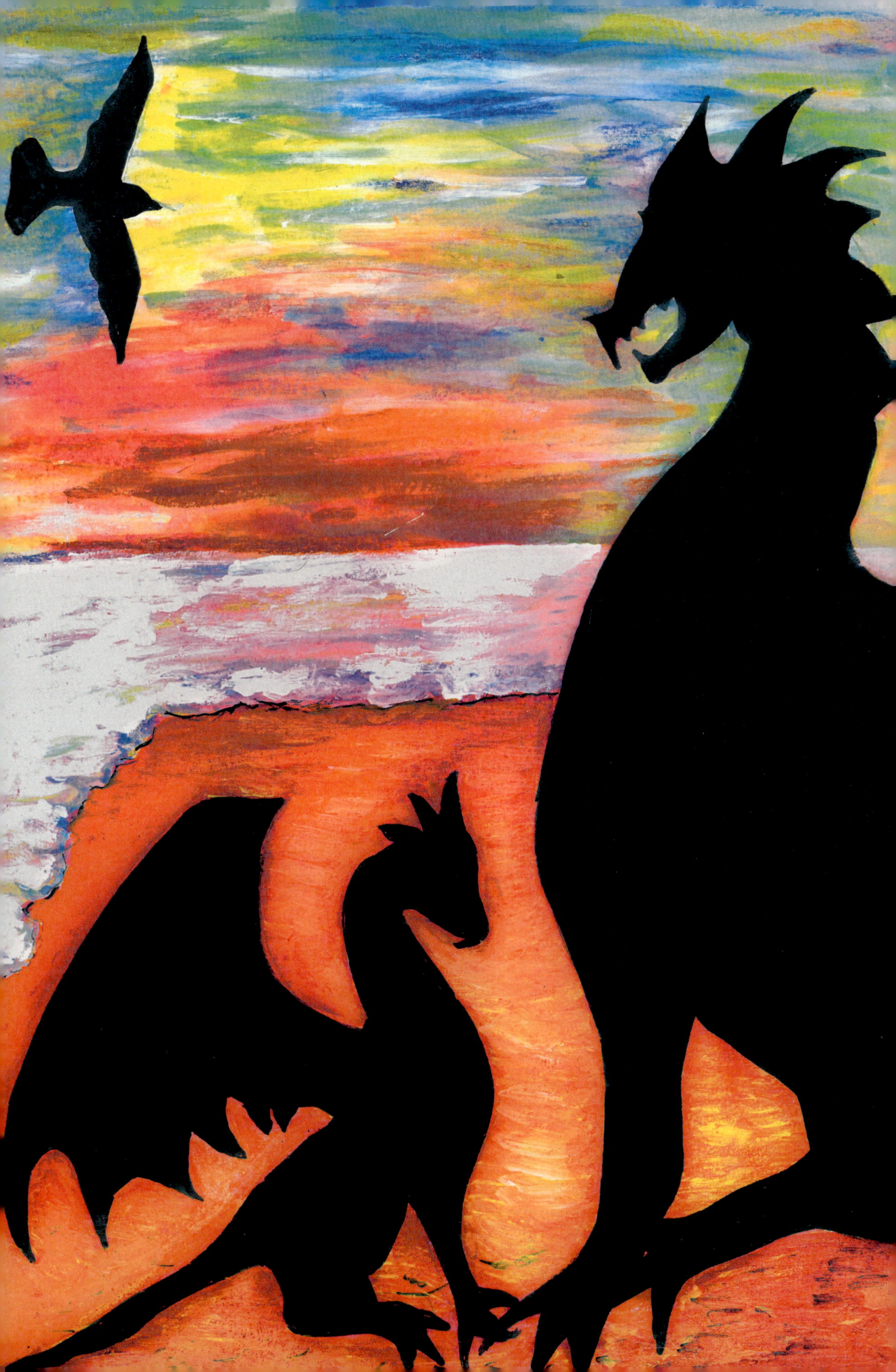

Facing Fear

Flynn looked longingly at the stars. He thought the stars astonishing, especially since his geography teacher taught him about constellations. He marvelled at the thought of how many light years away the stars were. How could it be that the light took so long to reach Earth? Some of the stars he gazed at no longer existed. Flynn often wondered what else lived in the illuminated skies above.

For thirteen years (his entire life, in fact), Flynn Mansell had lived in a small flat in London with his mother, Patsy, and his sister Barbara. Yet London had never felt like home. It was such a busy place, full of people, noise and an endless stream of traffic. People rarely walked anywhere just for pleasure, or to be in the moment. Life here was chaotic and hectic.

Flynn had an enormous empathy for animals. He was never allowed to keep pets in the flat - not that it stopped him! He once hid Houdini the hamster in his clothes cupboard. His mum had noticed bits of sawdust on the carpet and so Houdini's discovery was imminent – but Flynn had managed to keep him hidden until Aunty Dana came to stay, at which point the furball lived up to his name and escaped. Screams of terror echoed through the hallway when the hamster crawled over her in bed one night.

After that, Flynn's mum gave Houdini away to the lady in the local chemist, which was probably just as well. Flynn had already taken Houdini to school and the hamster had escaped there too. Hidden in his bedroom, he still had his sticklebacks in jars, cardinal beetles in matchboxes and a pair of white mice in his desk. He'd learnt to make sure there was never any trace of sawdust or seeds. He wasn't going to get caught a second time.

Once on a week-long school trip Flynn even managed to sneak a black German shepherd dog called Sam into his dormitory. He had felt terribly sorry for Sam. The owner appeared to never have time for him, and would talk to Sam gruffly. Each night the dog would wander up the fire escape barking for Flynn to open the back door. One miserable, wet evening Flynn's teacher came to ask if anyone had seen Sam. Flynn shook his head, trying not to glance down at the wet paw prints on the floor. He wondered if his teacher knew he was lying. If she did, she never let on.

Flynn's haven was London Zoo. From home it was a thirty-minute stroll through the park and along the canal, which ran parallel to the zoo. Flynn never had enough money for a ticket. When nobody was looking he would sneak over the black metal railings and alight on the long grass by the huge bird house. Although he loved the place, he didn't like seeing birds in cages. Birds, he felt, were born to fly, not to be trapped behind bars. He would disappear quickly to the other side of the zoo through the tunnel that ran under the road. This area housed lions, tigers, pandas and so many other magical creatures.

Fascinated by the reptile house, Flynn loved to watch the huge pythons that hung around the zookeeper's neck. If he was lucky, he would sometimes get to hold one. He spent hours observing the iguanas that tasted the air with their blue tongues, and listening to the chirping crickets echoing in the antiquated building.

When school days approached, Flynn would look in the fridge for something to make his packed lunch with. Usually, he would spread Marmite on bread and garnish the sandwiches with watercress. In truth, he was not very keen on his culinary creation, but there wasn't much else to choose from.

Flynn was lucky that his school was on the other side of Regent's Park. It meant he could wander through nature before the mad rush of the school day. As he ambled through the park, he would often strike up a conversation with his friend Karam, and Karam's faithful companion Tolle. Tolle was a large brown dog whose amber eyes followed Karam's every move.

Karam had lived in the park for many years. In winter he wore layers of jumpers underneath his scruffy brown overcoat. In the summer he wore a fragrant pink carnation in his coat buttonhole. His long, wispy grey hair was always covered by a cap. Whenever he saw Flynn he would give a toothless grin and hand him a mint humbug. Flynn knew that he must never take a sweet from a stranger, but he had known Karam most of his life and they had developed a firm friendship.

It was Flynn's mum who had first spoken to Karam. She wanted to teach Flynn how important it was to respect everyone, however they looked. She said people were like a patchwork quilt, different and colourful, and everybody had the ability to enrich the tapestry of life.

Flynn and Karam would talk endlessly about things that interested them both. Sometimes it would be about the stars and planets, or even the bold seagulls snatching a sandwich from their hands. They would chatter about how Karam had rescued Tolle when she was a puppy.

Once and only once, Karam talked about escaping from his war-torn country. Head bowed in his hands, he mentioned how his family had perished. Flynn could sense the gaping hole in his heart. He understood why Tolle meant so much to the old man.

One day as Flynn was walking towards his friend, he sensed something was terribly wrong. As he got closer, he saw that Karam was physically shaking and weeping inconsolably. "Whatever is the matter?" cried Flynn. His stomach lurched as he noticed the brown dog was nowhere to be seen.

"Tolle has disappeared!" wailed Karam. "She was chasing leaves one minute and the next she was gone. Tolle never leaves my side. I have searched everywhere. I don't know what to do."

"I will search for her; she can't have gone too far." He set off on his usual walk across the park. Flynn tried to feel her presence, but he couldn't.

He felt empty and slumped down on a tree stump. As he did this, he heard a tiny voice saying, "You won't find her sitting there." At first, Flynn thought he imagined it, but the voice came again only with more urgency. "Get up, you lazy boy, Tolle needs you!" Looking on the ground Flynn saw a tiny beetle waving its antennae. It's not possible, he thought. With that, the beetle started to make the long journey up Flynn's trouser leg and on to his shoulder.

"Do you know where she is?" whispered a rather perplexed Flynn to the little beetle.

"Yes, Sven the goblin has captured her!"

"A goblin?" laughed Flynn. "Be serious."

"I am," replied the beetle. "You talk about being serious? You are conversing with a beetle."

This made sense. Flynn decided to wonder about the talking beetle later and deal with the problem of Tolle's whereabouts now. "What does a goblin want with Tolle?"

"To eat her, of course!" cried the beetle. "It can't be allowed to happen! She has been a Keeper all her life!"

Flynn had no idea what a Keeper was, but he felt it must be important. "Please tell me where she is," he said quickly.

To which the beetle replied…

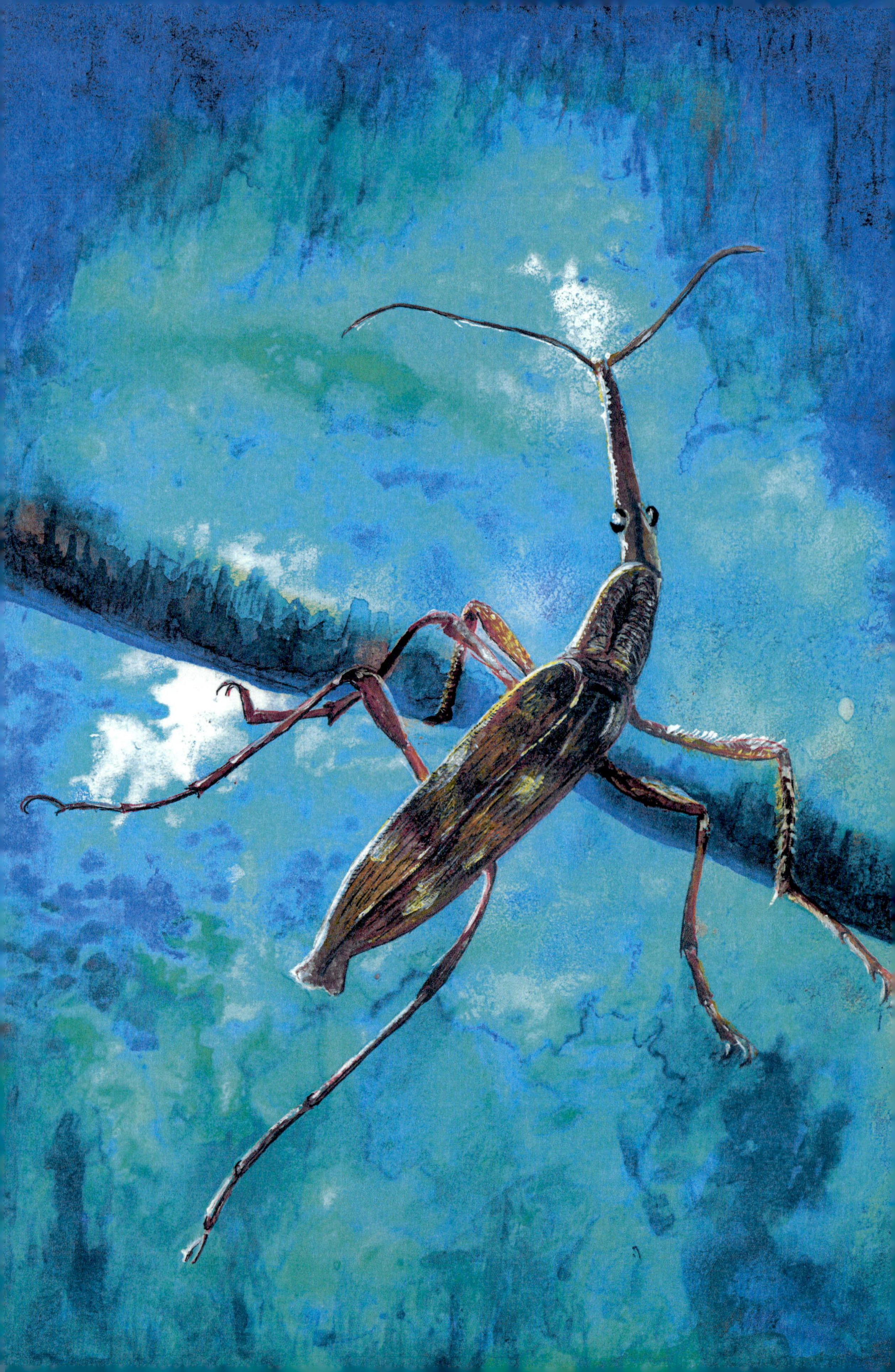

"The beautiful Keeper, her paws thus tied
The Goblin trapped her and told her lies
She can be found in a world underground
Where nothing is heard, not a single sound
The dark flowing water is not clear
You must go now, don't show your fear.

She is held in a tunnel near the cage
Where enclosed animals pace with rage
The Goblin is ugly and covered in mud
It is necessary for you to shed your blood
The brick-built tunnel connects the portal
For you to find, a mere earth-bound mortal.

Know thyself so very well
For only YOU can break his spell
Show the Goblin his shadow self
This will bring forth his light and wealth
Look into his thoughts, and his eyes
It is here you'll discern truth from lies.
Move forward on your journey, courageous Seeker
Return our brave and powerful Keeper."

Flynn groaned. "How am I meant to work out this riddle? Please just tell me where she is!" But as he looked around, Flynn realised the beetle had vanished. He let out a long, despondent sigh. He asked himself. Found beneath the ground, what kind of useless clue is that? If it is somewhere that doesn't have sound, maybe she is trapped in a vault? And - what on Earth is a Keeper?

Flynn scanned the landscape repeating the line, "The dark flowing water is not clear." The lake in front of me is murky, he thought, but it doesn't flow. He could feel his frustration growing. He decided to find Karam and see if he would believe him. Karam was nowhere to be seen.

As Flynn walked, his mind became more focused. There is other water, he thought suddenly... the canal. It flows brown! What was the verse again? Something about a cage... and in that instant, he knew Tolle was being held in the zoo. With quickening speed he set off through Regent's Park towards Camden Lock Canal.

For the second time that day Flynn climbed over the metal fence. Earlier the railings seemed exciting, but in the dark, they felt cold and menacing. The spikes threatened to impale him if he slipped. He had to make sure he was balanced not only in body but mind as well.

The zoo looked so different. Many of the animals seemed to be staring expectantly at Flynn. There was an owl with one eye transfixed on him. The owl seemed to give him a wink. Flynn heard the roar of a lion and the grunt of a wild boar. Where to now, he pondered, pacing around the enclosures.

An okapi glared at him and mewed, "Hey boy, what are you doing, disturbing our peace?"

"I am looking for Sven the goblin," answered Flynn.

"You are looking for the goblin?... are you sure you want to find him?" shuddered the okapi. "The only friends he has are silent ones. Many 'friends' have visited him and never returned."

Flynn's legs started to shake. He was beginning to feel very nervous. "He has captured Tolle, my friend's dog. I need to get her back."

"Good luck with that," replied the okapi sarcastically. "I hope your friend is worth all this trouble. You will find Sven where the tunnel meets the portal." The okapi turned its back and trotted away.

Flynn shook himself and wondered if there was something wrong with him. Surely it wasn't normal to be hearing animals talk? Another thought occurred to him... what if everyone was supposed to understand animals? What if these precious animals' lives had been changed because people didn't listen to them, so they stopped talking to us?

The only tunnel Flynn could think of was the one that connected the north side of the zoo to the south side. It must be this one. Flynn ran as fast as his legs could carry him towards the tunnel. Once again he heard the roar of a lion as if the lion was spurring him on. Breathe deeply: s-l-o-w deep breaths, Flynn told himself.

As he approached the tunnel he could feel an unusual energy spiralling around him. It made him feel sick and dizzy. The line of the verse the beetle recited about shedding blood was really beginning to worry him.

Flynn placed his fingers on the wall and felt the cold dampness of the bricks. He moved his hands slowly trying to find a doorway in the dark. About halfway along, he felt a brick jutting out.

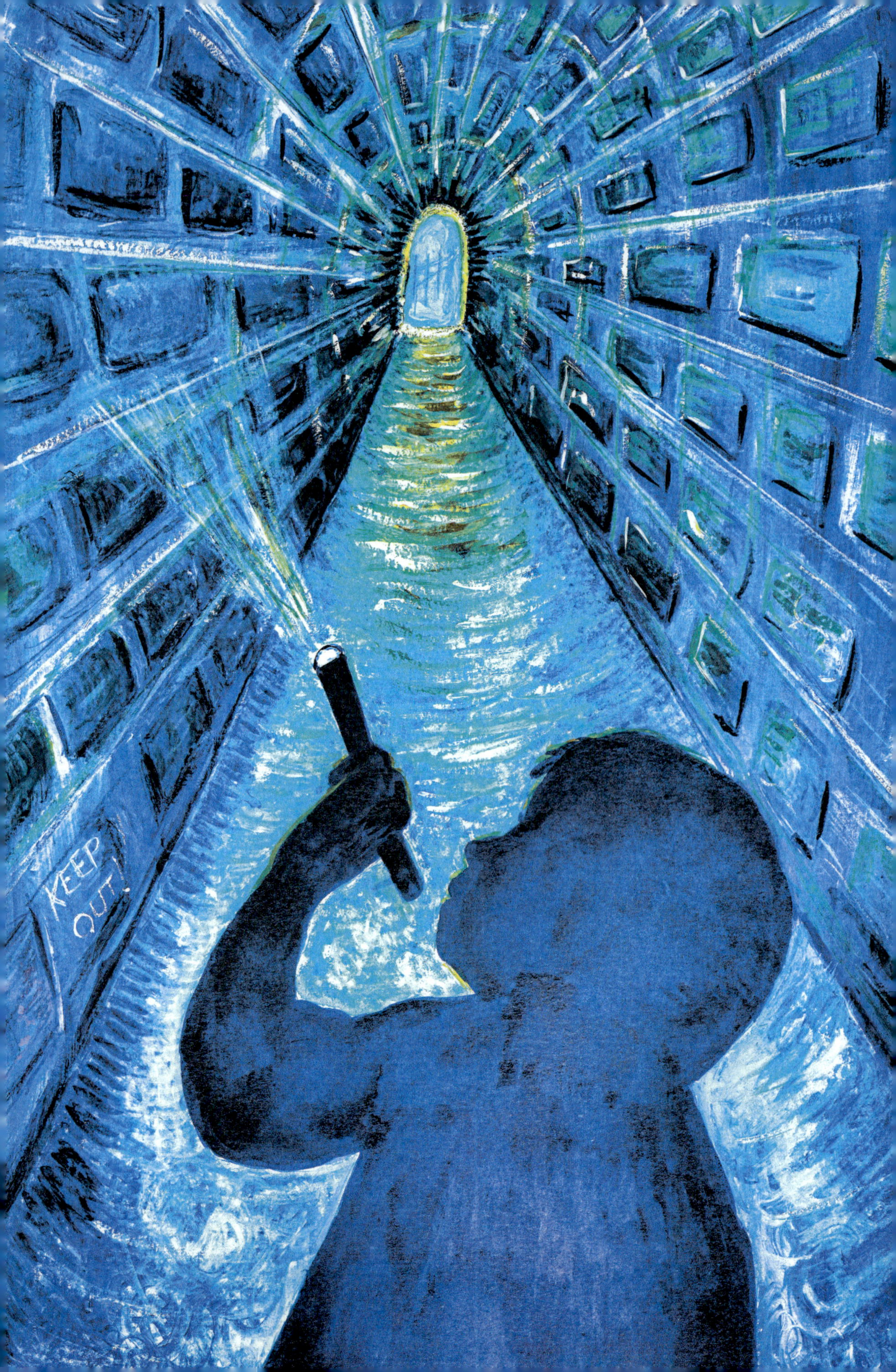
KEEP OUT

It was sharp and Flynn cut his finger. The wound was deep. As his blood dripped on to the floor, a portal opened underneath his feet. Flynn lost his balance and tumbled down an underground staircase.

The stairwell was dark and lifeless. Dim yellow lanterns lined the walls. It was eerily silent. The air was so cold it took Flynn's breath away. A stench of rotting meat assaulted his nostrils and a feeling of complete despair made him want to run, but he pressed on. Down and down Flynn crept, navigating the slippery stone stairs. He tried to steady his nerves by counting the steps. There were 111. Flynn could feel his heart pounding.

As he reached the bottom step he saw a pair of arched wooden doors. Grasping the iron handles he pushed with all his might. The heavy doors opened. The stench overwhelmed him. Thinking he might be sick, he swallowed hard to try to push down the contents of his stomach. As he looked up, Flynn was horrified to see the most menacing beast imaginable.

The creature was about four feet tall. Batlike ears framed his wizened face. His eyes looked empty and soulless. Sharp teeth hung from his mouth like ornate jewellery. The goblin was hunched with gnarled fingers. Every ounce of Flynn's body wanted to scream, but he knew he must hide his terror and disgust from the goblin.

The goblin was surrounded by hideous creatures of all shapes and sizes. The entities oozed dread, and menacing lifelessness emanated from their bodies. Mournful noises echoed around the rock walls. Vines hung from the low ceilings, like tentacles trying to swallow him. "How dare you come to the Kingdom of Sven uninvited!" bellowed the goblin.

Panic started to engulf Flynn, but he managed to respond calmly. "I have come to take Tolle home."

"What?" sneered the goblin, "Everything I have is mine. I own it all, the whole Kingdom is mine. Even the wretched creatures that I allow to share my dwelling are mine!"

"You have stolen my friend and I have come to take her back," Flynn said forcefully.

"Who are you talking about? There are no humans here," growled the goblin.

"She is a dog," replied Flynn, looking straight into the goblin's empty eyes.

"A dog... what do you mean, a dog?" screamed Sven. "Animals are not important to humans."

"What makes you think that?" asked Flynn, trying to hide the anger in his voice.

"You humans deforest the land so animals lose their homes. You restrict their freedom and place them in cramped cages for human pleasure. You invite some animals into your homes to love and cherish and others you breed to eat. You cannot tell me that an old dog has any value to anyone. She is of no use to you, but she will give me a hearty meal," retorted the goblin as he licked his lips and rubbed his filthy clawed hands together.

"No! Tolle is much loved. Yes, humans have made many errors and have damaged the land and the seas we depend upon, but many are now working to right the wrongs we've done. There is a change coming!" replied Flynn passionately.

"Hmm. What does the dog offer the human?" questioned Sven offhandedly.

"Tolle means the world to my friend. She is his Keeper and his family. Offering warmth and comfort when he is cold and lonely. A faithful companion who listens to all his worries without judgement. Tolle is the reason he gets up each morning," replied Flynn.

"This is my Kingdom and you can't have her," hissed the goblin, jumping up and down in rage. "You should leave now whilst you still have a chance."

"I will not leave her behind," responded Flynn, as he gazed directly into the goblin's eyes.

Sven had never had anyone or anything refuse an order, let alone look deeply into his eyes. It made him feel unsettled. No one had ever dared to question him. What was this magic the boy held? It made him appear without fear. Whatever it was, the goblin wanted it.

Sven was growing old. The only way he could make the creatures in his Kingdom follow his commands was by threatening them with evil acts. He broke their spirits by separating them from their friends and families. By withholding food and continually telling them they didn't need to think for themselves. He fed them lies about how he was saving them. But he was using them for his own benefit. They served his purpose.

Sven scratched his bristly chin thoughtfully. "Very well. I will let you take the wretched beast - on one condition. You must agree to return before the next full Moon. You will bring with you that which you treasure most. If you fail or lie to me, I will hunt you down and destroy all that is precious to you, including the dog! Do we have a deal?"

"Y-yes," stammered Flynn.

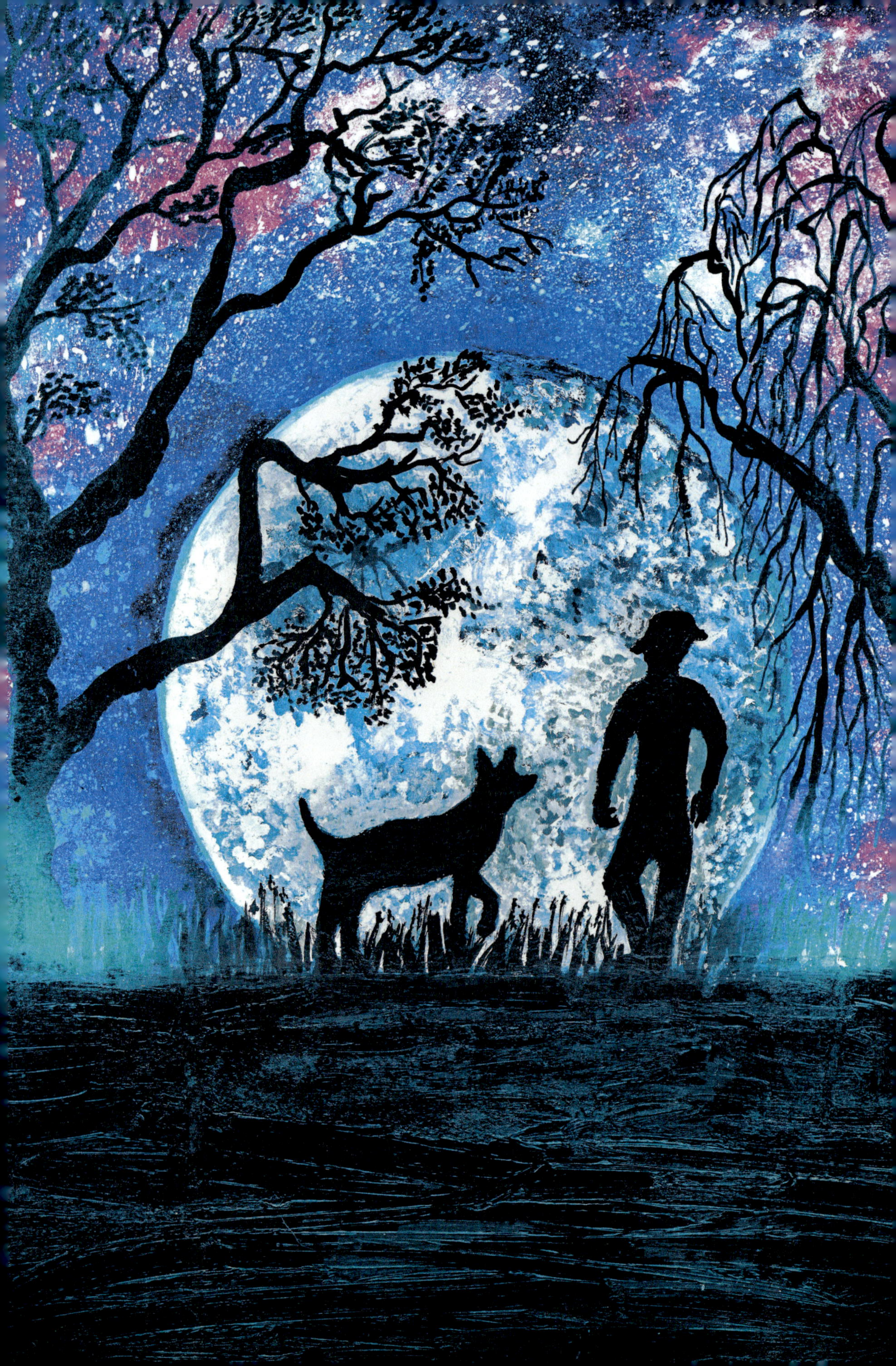

With that, Sven ordered his creatures to go and untie Tolle and bring her to the boy. When Tolle saw Flynn, her dull eyes lit up with joy. She bounded over to him, jumped around his legs and licked his hands and face, her tail wagging all the while with sheer delight at seeing her friend again.

The goblin looked on in amazement. He couldn't understand what he was witnessing. Sven had never seen so much happiness and unconditional love before. He felt confused as the dog and boy held on to each other, lost in the moment of their reunion.

"Thank you, Sven," said Flynn, keeping Tolle close to him. "I will return before the next full Moon." With Tolle by his side, Flynn ran up the stairs two at a time. He could hear the goblin screaming...

"Don't forget our deal. Don't try and trick me. I will know if you are lying!"

Breathing heavily, Flynn found the nearest turnstile out of the zoo. Tolle followed. Within minutes they were back in the park. This was the first time Flynn had walked through the park at night. His mind was racing. What would Sven accept? What would happen if he didn't like what Flynn gave him? He didn't doubt that the goblin would find him and make him into a hearty meal.

Walking past the lake Flynn watched the swans gliding across the still waters. Everything felt surreal. Flynn could feel Tolle's pace quickening until she was almost running. Mmm... she can sense Karam, thought Flynn. Karam was sitting on a bench staring into space. Tolle jumped onto his lap and nuzzled him. Karam burst into happy tears.

"Oh my beautiful friend, where have you been? Are you hurting, my darling?" he cried.

Flynn sat next to Karam and wondered what he should tell his friend. Karam sensed Flynn's hesitancy and calmly waited for his friend to decide to speak, and in the end Flynn told him everything. It felt good to talk. His friend neither laughed nor told him what to do. Instead he simply said that he believed in Flynn. That Flynn had the power inside of him to find a solution. Karam would stand by his side and together they would confront the goblin.

Although Flynn felt comfort in his friend's words, he felt scared of the path that lay ahead. "I know that the goblin is frightening," muttered Flynn to Karam. "But the rhyme the beetle recited stated that only I could break his spell. I feel this is something I need to do alone. What I really would like to know is what a Keeper is."

"I have no idea," replied Karam. "But if you can talk to animals, maybe one of our friends in the park might know." With that, a magnificent tawny owl swooped down from a tree and landed on the grass in front of Flynn.

The winking owl, thought Flynn, crouching down to the owl's level. "Do you know what a Keeper is?" he asked.

The owl hooted noisily, "A Keeper is a guardian, protector and bodyguard. A Keeper watches over you in your hour of need. Everyone has a Keeper." Wow! thought Flynn, that's exactly what Tolle is.

Flynn asked the owl another question. "The beetle said I was a Seeker. What is a Seeker?"

"A Seeker," squawked the owl, "faces the daunting Universe with a valiant vulnerability and courageous openness. A Seeker does not follow the herd like sheep but questions what is seen and unseen. A Seeker has a deep connection to truth and although they feel fear, that does not stop them from facing it."

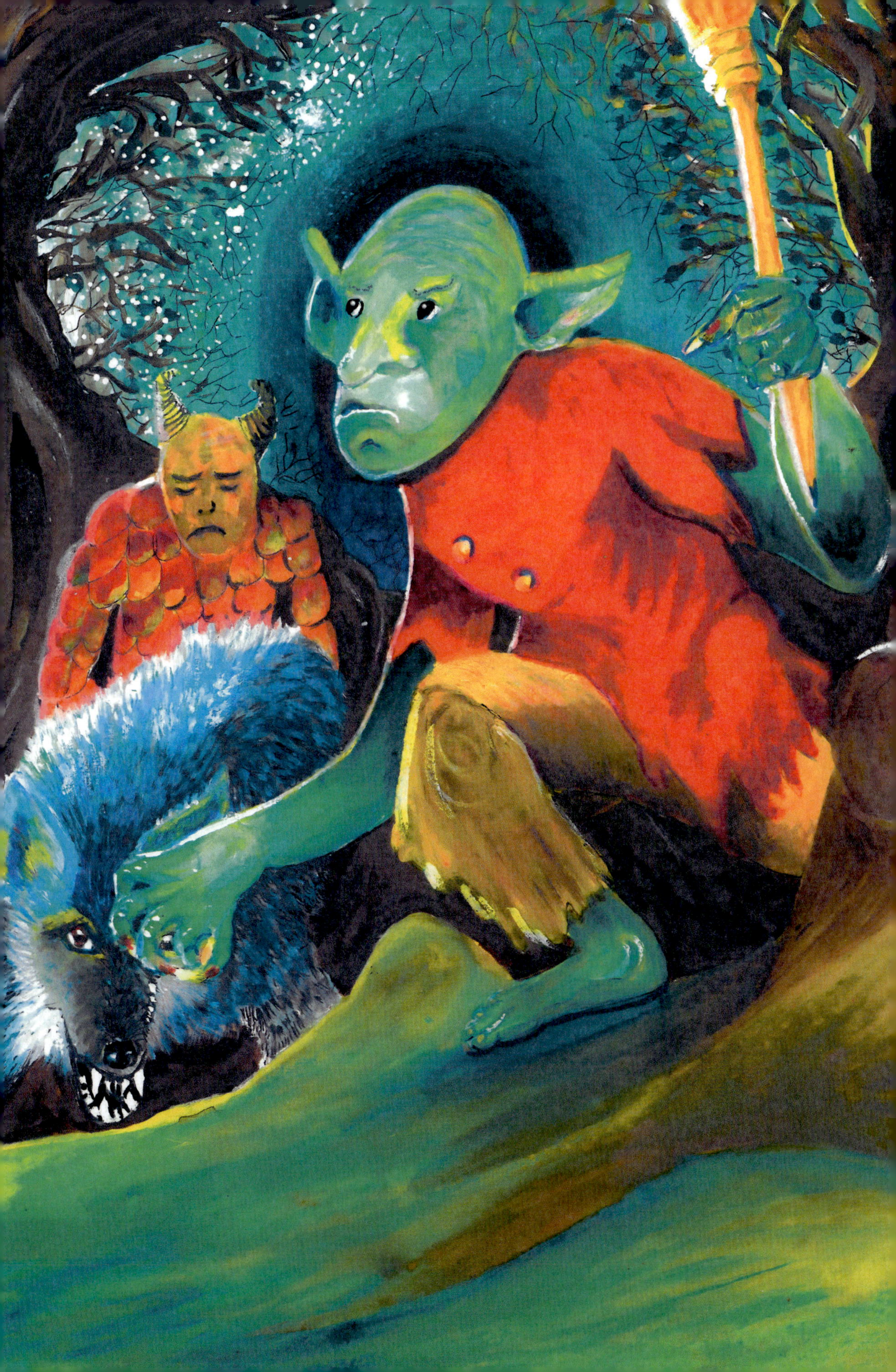

"That can't be me. The beetle must have been mistaken," muttered Flynn.

"Why do you say that?" hooted the tawny.

"I am scared. I don't think I have the courage to face the goblin again," whispered Flynn with despair.

"Oh, but you do, you have faced fear," hooted the wise owl. "Look what you have done already. Remember, you are never truly alone and sometimes power comes from unlikely places." With a swish of his tail, the owl flew high into the night sky.

For the next few evenings the Moon was waxing, and Flynn had an image of a sand timer running out. He thought of the owl's words... 'Remember you are never alone.' He made a list of all the things that were precious to him. His mum, his sister, Karam, his mice. Going for walks in the park, listening to music and laughter. None of these things he felt the goblin would value as he did. He and Sven were literally worlds apart.

A sudden thought occurred to Flynn... what if Sven didn't value these things simply because he had never experienced them? All the goblin knew was anger, loneliness and greed. What if Flynn could teach him about love, companionship and generosity of spirit? Flynn recognised that humans have two sides; maybe a goblin did too. A side that you show to the outside world and a side that is often buried deep inside.

Sven was resentful, and unappreciative of his Kingdom. Characteristics that the goblin thought served him well - but in truth, they imprisoned him in a world of darkness. Perhaps I can help him find his light, Flynn thought excitedly.

Without thinking further Flynn decided to return to Sven. He wasn't sure yet what he was going to say and he certainly didn't have anything to take... or did he? The night air was once again cold and he sensed the stillness of the animals in the zoo. It was almost as if they were holding their breath waiting for an outcome.

Flynn felt his way until he reached the wonky brick. Once again the sharpness cut his skin and blood leeched out onto the ground. The portal opened. This time Flynn was ready for it. Breathing deeply he started his descent into the underworld.

The stench assaulted Flynn's senses once more, as he opened the heavy arched doors. There before him the goblin sat on a golden throne encrusted with precious stones. An assortment of creatures cowered nearby in the shadows, their eyes begging to be saved from the life they found themselves trapped in.

"Well, where is it, the thing you treasure most?" thundered Sven, noticing Flynn's empty hands.

"It's right here," beckoned Flynn as he placed his hand on his heart.

"What is this fraud? I see only emptiness!" hollered Sven.

"I am most precious to ME," replied Flynn. "For if I do not value myself or have a true heart, I cannot be of service to others."

"You have brought me nothing, you have tricked me!" screamed the goblin.

"I have not tricked you. I am here. I am valuable if you choose to see me for who I really am," replied Flynn.

The goblin was confused. "Do you mean I now own you?" cried Sven.

"I am here, and will work for you, but you can never own my soul. For that is mine and mine alone. I give to you freely all that I am," whispered Flynn.

"Freely?" sneered the goblin. "That's not how it works. No one stays here through choice."

"Why not?" asked Flynn.

"Because I make them stay here through fear."

"It doesn't need to be like that," replied Flynn, shaking his head sadly.

"I know no other way," said Sven, scratching his head.

"I can teach you," smiled Flynn.

"It's too late," mumbled the goblin sadly. "I am too old to learn."

Flynn could see a glimmer of light. The goblin held no real power at all; it was just an illusion. An illusion that the creatures in his Kingdom helped perpetuate with their own feelings of anxiety. A mass consciousness of fear that every soul fed on.

Flynn pulled out a small shiny object from his trouser pocket. The goblin glanced suspiciously, screwed up his eyes and spat, "What is that?"

"This is a mirror; take a look, if you would like to."

The goblin peered into the mirror and was shocked at what he saw. Sunken skin and soulless eyes snarled angrily at him. "Who is this dreadful creature?" he cried. "I do not recognise him. What is this deceit?"

"This, my friend, is you! Can you see your anger and frustrations? The mirror reflects back what you project."

Sven fell to his knees. He saw something that frightened him even more than his own reflection. He saw death. He realised this was no way to live. "Please help me," begged the goblin. "Not because I command you to, but because I would like to learn from you."

Flynn nodded; he knew he had managed to chisel away a little bit of the barrier that surrounded the goblin's heart. "Of course. Have you noticed? You have already started to help yourself," whispered Flynn. "There is growth in asking for help and in making mistakes, if we learn from our actions."

"How can I be a leader without controlling through fear? I am weak and old, no one will listen to me," wept the goblin.

"You may be right. You might not be able to control your people, only time will tell. They need a leader, not a prison guard." Flynn spoke quietly. "Can you continue in this cycle of darkness?"

"No!" wailed Sven. "I can't go on with this loneliness. It eats away at me. I need a Keeper like Tolle. Will you be my Keeper?"

"Sven, that is not my role. I think Keepers come from a different realm. They watch over us and appear when they are most needed," sighed Flynn, surprised when the knowledge appeared suddenly in his mind. "What I can promise you is that if you are truthful to yourself and let go of your fear, nothing will seem as bad as it does in this present moment. You will find freedom. Perhaps you will rediscover a part of you long forgotten about. You may even discover who your Keeper is. Everyone has one," said Flynn kindly.

Flynn watched in amazement as the heavily lined features of the goblin changed. He looked younger and his soulless eyes began to sparkle. The air felt less dense. There was a feeling of optimism. Flynn knew that a great change was coming.

Sven nodded his head as if he could read Flynn's thoughts. "I think you are very special," said Sven. "Please come and visit me when you are passing."

"I would like that," laughed Flynn. "Not because you have asked me, but because I want to." Flynn took out a box of matches from his pocket and a small candle. As he struck the match and lit the candle a grin appeared on the goblin's face.

"You did bring me magic after all!" he cried.

"Yes," smiled Flynn. "Remember that no matter how much darkness there is around you, a little light can banish the shadows."

"It is late, you must be on your way," said Sven.

Flynn's face lit up. The spell had been broken. There seemed to be an understanding between him and Sven; perhaps even the start of a friendship. They both had their freedom, as important as life itself.

***

"I thought Flynn was really brave facing the goblin on his own! Do you think he was born brave, or did he learn how to be brave?" Darion asked Iridiana.

"Wow, that's a deep question. I believe we are all born without fear. Each day we face choices that will challenge us. These challenges can help us grow braver, but equally they can make us afraid and distract us from being who we really are."

"Flynn stood up to the evil goblin and saved his friend. True friendship is a precious gift," said Darion thoughtfully. "I am going to try and be a better friend. If the Earth Dragons are cruel to Skywing tomorrow, I will stand with him," Darion said adamantly.

"I am very pleased to hear you say that. Taking the path less travelled is hard, yet more meaningful. You were brave when you admitted your mistake. That took real courage. "Tomorrow you may need to find that courage again," smiled Iridiana, full of admiration for her nephew.

"I will, Aunt Iridiana. But for now, I am hungry," chuckled Darion.

"Well, we better get back to the broth!" replied Iridiana. With that, the two dragons took off and glided over the forests and mountains towards home.

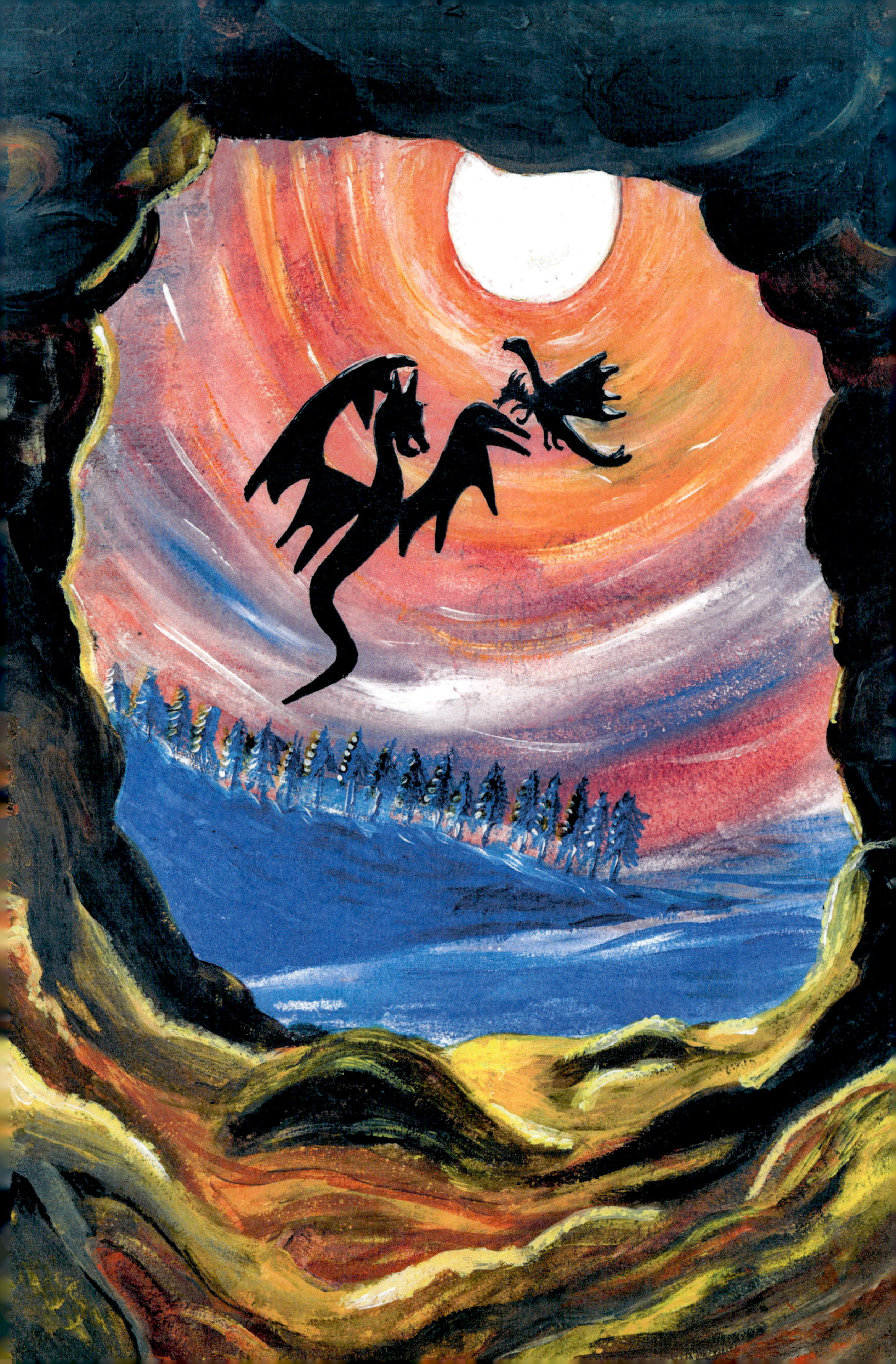

Unconditional Love

When Darion flew home from training, his face was beaming. His whole body was surrounded by an exquisite purple glow. Finding it difficult to contain his excitement, he lolloped over to his aunt and gave her the biggest smile she had ever seen.

"Guess what?" he shouted.

"Oh please tell," grinned Iridiana.

"I was given the best gift today," laughed Darion.

"What was it?" asked his aunt, wondering what gift could possibly have made Darion quite so happy.

"I have a new friend and she shares the same interests as me," replied Darion.

"Is your friend, Skywing?"

"No... not Skywing, although I did apologise to him. My friend is called Phoenix. She is a Fire Dragon and we joined forces. Phoenix is great at lighting fires, but not so good at putting them out! We complement each other, and I think we are going to have a lot of fun together," smiled Darion with a cheeky grin.

"You mean you are going to get up to lots of mischief," chuckled his aunt.

"Yes!" giggled Darion. "Phoenix accidentally set fire to the cloud ball when she sneezed! Luckily I was flying behind her and I put it out! Together we helped our team win the Cloud Ball Tournament."

"Winning the tournament must have felt like such an achievement," said his aunt.

"Not really. I was happier about having someone to talk to than actually winning!"

"I think you won all round," smiled Iridiana. "Are you up for another story?"

"Definitely… but you must be running out of gifts by now," said Darion, curling up in a ball next to the warm fire.

"We'll have to see about that," said his aunt playfully. "This is a tale about two Earthling children."

***

Blowing warm air into her freezing hands Maddie was determined to get her fingers working again. She'd had such a busy morning helping her Dad feed the lambs that her hands felt like ice blocks. Maddie's brother James leaned out of the kitchen window. "Do you want a hot chocolate?" he shouted.

"Definitely!" groaned Maddie. "I need to warm up." Balancing the hot chocolate on his bike, James manoeuvred around piles of straw and mud, making his way to the barn. Panting, Maddie collapsed on a hay bale and eagerly sipped the warm drink.

"Have you nearly finished feeding the lambs?" asked James with a cheeky grin.

"Why?" answered Maddie suspiciously.

"I saw the white squirrel climb the oak tree and she hasn't come back. I really want to know where she goes," James replied.

"Sounds like a plan," laughed Maddie, looking happily towards the ancient oak tree that stood alone in the middle of the cattle field. A curtain of fog was draped over the tree's heavy boughs.

For years her parents had made up stories about the pedunculate oak. They even named her - Majesty. The tree had been growing for at least a thousand years. Gnarled bark had grown into the shapes of animals and mythical beasts. Maddie often ran her hands over its trunk, feeling the oak's rough texture. The magnificent tree was covered with emerald moss. Fragile lichen hung from her limbs like silk.

"Come on Maddie, drink up!" shouted James impatiently.

Maddie slurped her drink and raced James to the tree. As James started to climb the oak, Maddie paused for a minute. She could hear James' voice echoing from somewhere above.

"Come on, slow coach!" he shouted.

"I'm coming," sighed Maddie, kicking off her wellington boots and leaving them at the base of the tree. "Wouldn't it be wonderful to see where she disappears to?" she called up to her brother.

Both children eagerly scrambled further up the oak in their quest to find the elusive white squirrel. The fog was becoming quite dense. It was impossible to tell how high Maddie and James had clambered. All that was visible below was the blanket of cloud. The higher they climbed, the cooler the air became. "I am not sure I want to go any further," shivered James. "I can't see my hands."

"We mustn't give up now," puffed Maddie. "We haven't found her."

Pushing on, the children came to a very thick covering of something that resembled white candy floss. "Awesome!" squealed James, gazing around excitedly. "We are on top of the world."

Maddie looked in awe. They were both floating in the clouds. James shrieked as he realised there was no gravity holding him down. Maddie did cartwheels. How free she felt. "What an amazing place!" she yelled, pinching herself to make sure she wasn't dreaming.

The vista was so much more colourful now that they had broken through the clouds. The warmth of the sun felt comforting. The air smelt fresh.

Just as Maddie was acclimatising, the temperature plummeted without warning, and the vibrant colours disappeared into complete darkness. The sun had vanished. It was as if they were entering the mouth of an expansive cave.

Maddie and James looked up to see a meteorite. It was enormous. It filled the entire sky, blocking the sun's rays. Both children could feel their bodies being drawn towards the gigantic floating rock. Scrabbling around, the two frightened siblings clung to each other and gripped Majesty's branches tightly. It was no use. The branches reluctantly let go of the precious cargo that dangled precariously from her fingertips. The power from this enormous rock drew them in, like a spider to its web. The children levitated through an opening. As the entrance closed, Maddie and James fell to the floor with a bump.

It wasn't a rock at all. It was a space station! There were buttons and screens everywhere. White corridors with shiny metal flooring could be seen in every direction and on multiple levels. The ship was immense. There were voices chattering all around. James felt a hand seize his jumper and pull him up.

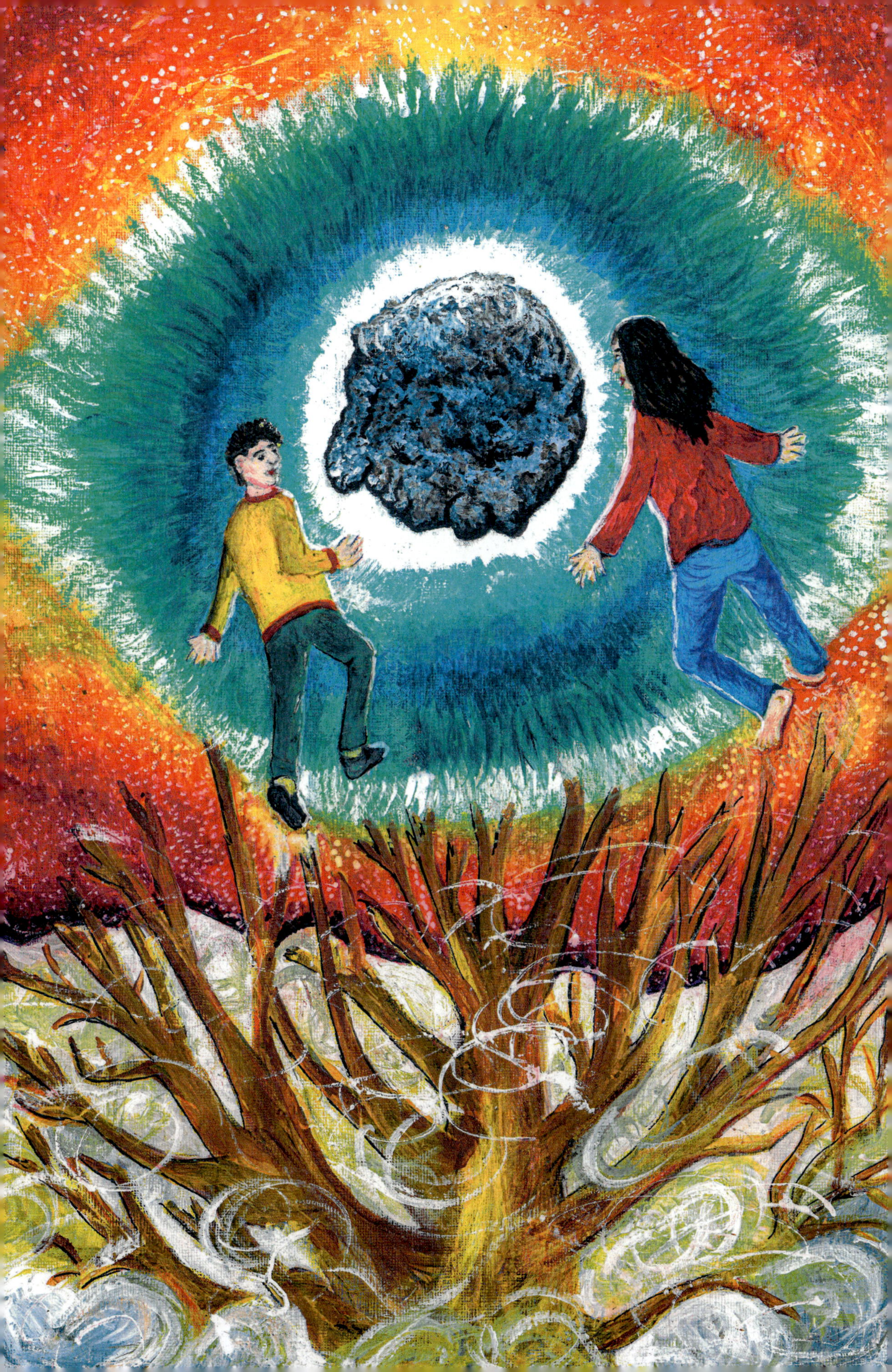

Another hand grabbed Maddie's sleeve, roughly dragging her to her feet. She could feel eyes watching them malevolently. The children stared at the red-haired being in front of them. He was perhaps seven feet tall, with piercing green eyes. "I see you have come to visit our Mothership," declared the Being.

"Not intentionally," replied Maddie nervously.

"W-we were just tree climbing," stammered James.

"I am not sure how you managed to find our Alpha Draconis star system. It should be impossible! Do you come from Terra?" enquired the Being.

"Terra?" muttered Maddie quietly. "We come from Earth."

"Same thing," replied the Being.

"We are sorry we have ended up on your ship, but we would really like to go back to our tree now," mumbled James, glancing quickly at his sister.

"You can't," responded the red-haired creature. "The portal is closed. You will stay with us until you are no longer of service."

"No!" wailed Maddie, "Our parents won't know where we are."

"Time is a human concept. Your parents will not notice you have gone," said the Being in a menacing voice.

"This is freaky," yelled James. "I want to go home."

Maddie reached out to James. She noticed the fear gripping him as his face turned ashen. She was worried that he would faint any minute. "Who are you?" cried Maddie.

"I am Raco. I am commander of the Toxicodons."

"Toxicodons?" repeated Maddie.

"Yes, we are a civilisation that governs the star system within the Draco Constellation," Raco said proudly. With that, the Being shapeshifted into a lizard-type creature. His mouth became very wide. Instead of pupils, his eyes now contained dark slits. Wings emerged from his spine.

"Please let us go," spluttered James, clinging tightly to his sister.

"Silence! Take them to the holding bay," shouted Raco in an icy voice.

James and Maddie were escorted by a wingless green and brown-skinned beast to a small airless room. As the door shut behind them they hugged each other. "This is terrible," sobbed James. "I just want to go home. These beings are scary."

"I know," whispered Maddie. "We will get home, James, I promise. We just need to work out how. Let's rest for a bit so that our minds can focus."

James was very tired from his ordeal. He leaned his back against the wall and found himself sliding down on to the floor. He rested his face in his hands and sobbed quietly to himself. Whilst his eyes were closed Maddie scanned the room. She felt around helplessly for anything that might assist their escape. There was nothing. Peering out of the tiny window she wondered how they would ever get home.

Suddenly, Maddie was aware of a scratching and gnawing sound. The noise was coming from outside the door. Small electrical explosions started to shoot out of the control panel on the wall. Without warning the door partially slid open and the white squirrel scampered inside. "Oh, thank you," cried Maddie in amazement. The little squirrel had chewed through the circuit board. "Come on." she whispered urgently as she gently shook James. "We need to get out of here!"

James saw the light streaming through the half-opened door and noticed the squirrel peering up at him. He held out his hand and gently stroked the squirrel's head. "Thanks, friend," he said, smiling.

Standing up quickly James squeezed through the door, carefully checking he wasn't being watched. Maddie followed, but she could only fit her head and shoulders through the gap. The rest of her body was tightly wedged. "James, you must go on without me," she ordered.

"I can't leave you here," cried James, tears trickling down his face.

"You must get out. Mum and Dad can't lose us both, now go!" barked Maddie, desperately wanting her brother to get to safety.

"No," replied James stubbornly. "We always do things together."

James looked carefully at the control panel in the door. The electronics were so different to anything he had learned at school, but he had nothing to lose. He connected two of the chewed wires together and was catapulted backwards as a huge spark lit up the room. A small explosion released the door a little more and Maddie was able to squeeze through.

"Are you OK?" asked Maddie.

"I am a bit shocked," replied James with a grin.

James's body was glowing. The glow spread over Maddie too and although they didn't understand what it was, it didn't seem to be doing them any harm.

Silently, they tiptoed along the corridor with the white squirrel following behind. As they approached an opened door they could hear hushed voices coming from inside. Maddie signalled to James to stand still. She crept forward, listening intently to what was being said.

Raco was talking. "We need to look into the pineal gland in the human brain whilst we have these children on board. It might help us understand why our plan to alter Earthling DNA is only working in some of the human population."

"Yes Commander, there seem to be different levels of consciousness amongst the Earthlings," responded a winged albino Toxicodon.

"If we are to gain complete control," continued Raco, "we need all humans to think in the same way. We must control their pineal glands."

With a sneer the Toxicodon snorted, "I wonder if they will ever realise that we have created the largest human prison on Terra, simply through mind manipulation." Maddie gasped. Surely this couldn't be right?

Without a sound, James and Maddie continued along the corridor, slipping past the unsuspecting Toxicodons. They crept towards the room where they had entered the Mothership.

James looked through a window. "I can't see Majesty," whispered James anxiously. "How are we going to get home?"

"I don't know, but I am not staying here while these toxic beings look inside our brains!" Maddie replied. The thought of it sent shivers down her spine.

The white squirrel began to behave strangely, running backwards and forwards to another door. I think she might be trying to tell us something!" exclaimed James excitedly. "Look!"

Through the door Maddie and James could see a small space craft. "That's it!" shouted Maddie breathlessly. "Our way home!"

Moving quickly, the two children entered the control room and managed to open the shuttle door. James glanced at the complicated control panel. "It won't work," he groaned in despair.

"What do you mean?" asked Maddie.

"Look - you need to press the launch button from the control pad to disengage the shuttle. I will push it. Take the squirrel with you."

"No," replied Maddie sternly. "We go together or not at all. There has to be another way."

With that the white squirrel climbed on to the control pad. "Of course," whispered Maddie. "Why didn't I think of that?" Maddie was reluctant to leave the squirrel behind, but she knew it was their only chance to escape. The squirrel looked at Maddie with knowing eyes. It almost seemed to be smiling at her, willing her to leave.

There were shouts in the corridors as an alarm bell rang out loudly. "Quick!" cried James. "Let's get out of here."

Maddie didn't need to be told twice. They buckled up and as the Toxicodons entered the control room the squirrel jumped onto the red button, launching the shuttle into space.

"Phew," sighed James. "That was too close for comfort! Have you any idea where we are heading?"

"No," replied Maddie. "I just pressed the autopilot button and trust that our path will take us where we are supposed to go. We have been looked after so far; don't you think?"

James had faith in his sister. He knew that she always thought of others. If anyone could get them out of this situation, Maddie could.

"I'm frightened, Maddie," whispered James.

"So am I," she replied. "But remember your power animal, and gain strength from him."

Maddie had taught James about power animals and how, if he was ever scared he should call them and ask for help. James's power animal was a badger. The animal represented not having to be big to be powerful and making your mark on the world. James' power animal aligned with him perfectly.

Maddie thought about her own power animal, the fox. This beautiful creature symbolised having the ability to move fast to overcome resistance and obstacles. This was certainly true of Maddie. She was a real warrior. From an early age, she had already fought many difficult battles.

Thinking back to the white squirrel she searched her mind for meaning. Of course, she thought. The white squirrel is the symbol of energy, playfulness and balance. It represents resourcefulness and trust. How wonderful that the squirrel had found them. Maddie only hoped the squirrel's cleverness would enable her to find her way home too.

The spaceship seemed to be travelling fast through space. Looking out the window was just like looking at a laser show. Bright lights lit up space in an explosion of radiance. After what seemed like hours the children became aware of the colourful lights fading. These were replaced with seven stars that emitted a glow not dissimilar to the glow around the children. Suddenly they felt the craft slow and descend downwards. No, not again, thought Maddie, as she tried to pilot the craft manually. The craft refused to deviate from its course.

Slowly, the shuttle descended to the ground. "Where are we?" asked James anxiously. "This doesn't look like Earth; the soil is too bright."

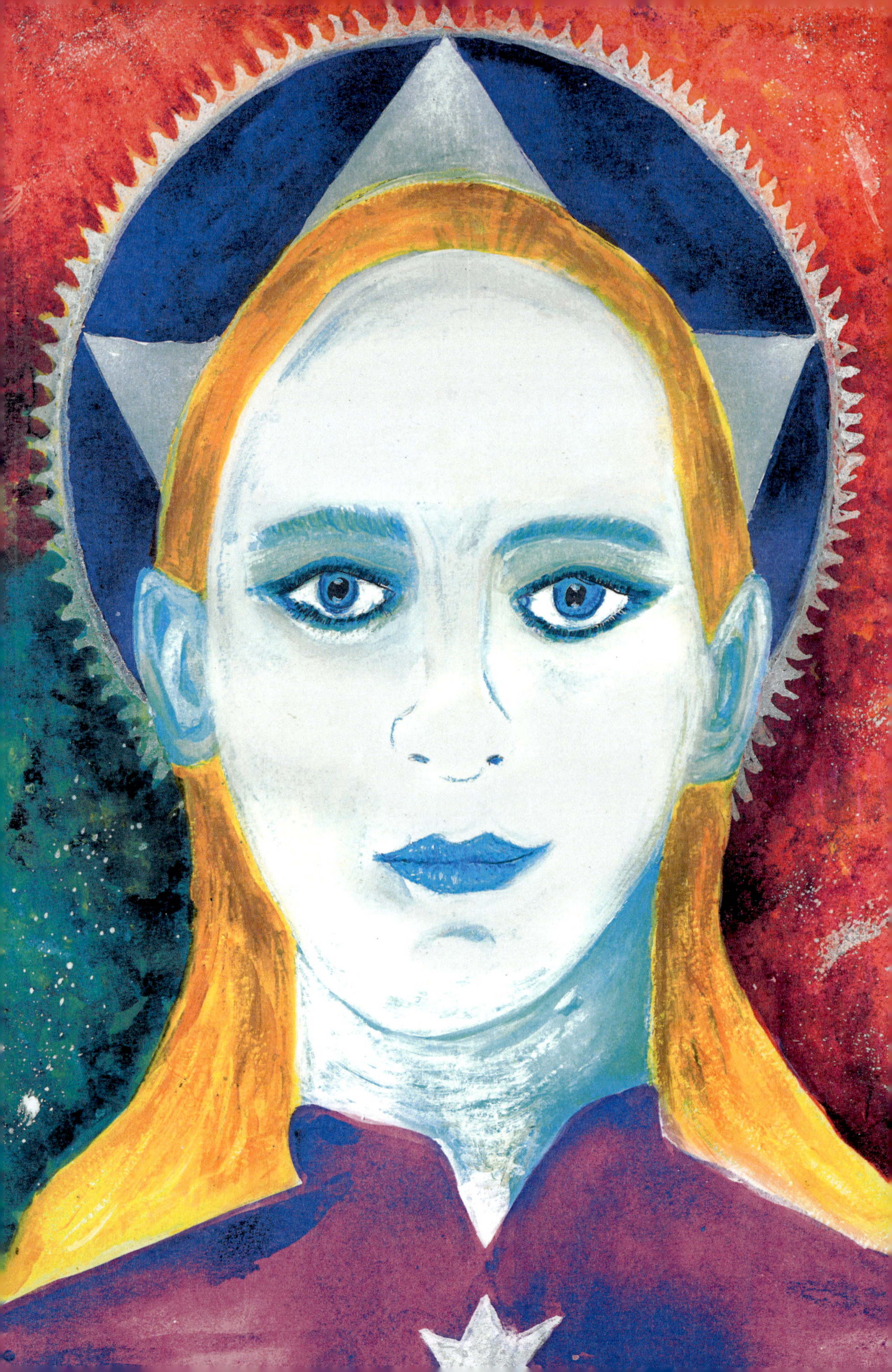

"I don't know. I didn't realise there was quite so much 'space' in space," replied a crestfallen Maddie.

Without warning the shuttle door opened to the unfamiliar planet. As Maddie and James stepped outside, they were greeted by beings that appeared almost human-like. Their bodies were tall and slender with a beautiful blue hue. Their facial features were symmetrical, with long foreheads. They appeared almost Nordic with bright blue eyes and blond hair. An air of calmness surrounded them.

"Welcome, Maddie and James, to Planet Erra. My name is Commander Fraxinus."

"How do you know our names?" asked James quizzically.

"We know all Earthling names, especially the old souls that we have met many times." smiled the commander. Please follow me, we have lots to catch up on."

The children followed the commander into a red building that looked like a large domed house. "You must be hungry after your long journey. Please sit down and eat."

"Actually, we would like to go home," replied Maddie forcefully, which startled James. He was starving and hoped his sister hadn't ruined his chance of something to fill his empty stomach.

"I understand your need to go back to your parents. I promise we will help you with that soon," smiled Fraxinus kindly. "On Earth only a few seconds have passed since you climbed the tree. Your parents will not worry because they do not know you are missing."

"How is that even possible?" muttered James shaking his head in disbelief.

"James, you have entered a different dimension, where time doesn't exist." explained Fraxinus. James nodded his head. He didn't completely understand, but he didn't wish to appear foolish.

"What is an 'old soul'?" asked Maddie quietly.

"An old soul," smiled Fraxinus, "is someone who has incarnated many times and has experienced much whilst living on Earth. They are often uninterested in what other people in their age group find exciting. You might say they don't fit in." This resonated with Maddie. Many of her friends were interested in the latest phone, or clothes. Maddie just loved walking and being surrounded by nature. She found it a waste of energy trying to be someone she wasn't.

"Why don't old souls fit in?" asked James, looking up from the plateful of exotic fruit laid out on the table beside him.

"Old souls understand what is important. They don't like to be part of silly quarrels. They have work to do. They are wise beyond their years," replied the commander.

Maddie smiled. "You are much kinder than those Toxicodon Beings. They were not... pleasant. They were creepy and... insidious."

"We, Bellator Luminis, are different. We watch closely over the Earth and try to help raise human consciousness. We act as guides and teachers. We only want the best for Planet Earth."

"Why do you help?" asked James, as he chewed enthusiastically on a strawberry-type fruit.

"Many moons ago we incarnated with the Earth and lived amongst you as a kind of experiment. There then came a time when it was felt humans needed to evolve on the Earth without our interference, so we left... although we didn't leave entirely. A spiritual leader remained for a while to watch over you and help with your evolution," replied Commander Fraxinus.

"The Toxicodons wanted to look at our DNA. Why was that?" enquired Maddie.

"The Toxicodons originally lived on Earth too," replied Fraxinus, "But after they mastered intergalactic travel they moved to Ferian, a planet in the Draco Constellations. Some Toxicodons decided to come back to Earth to try and alter human DNA."

"Why would they want to do that?" asked Maddie.

"They want to rule the Earth so that they can feel powerful. The Toxicodons felt that by restricting the human brain, they would be able to put a limit on human consciousness and control how humans thought."

"But how can they get control?" asked James, somewhat alarmed.

"These beings have power over every single country, and so have created a global prison," said Fraxinus calmly. "We, the warriors of light, are assisting the Earth to help you."

"I overheard the Toxicodons talking about a human prison!" murmured Maddie. "But how is Earth a prison? I don't understand?"

"The prison was created by drawing borders between vast areas of land. This led to endless wars between divided countries. The leaders of these countries were greedy, and wanted power over each other. Think of all the unnecessary wars that rage on."

"Yes, conflicts are terribly sad," replied Maddie solemnly.

"Another weapon used to control human minds is the media," continued Fraxinus.

"How can that be a weapon?" asked James in amazement. "I love using my phone and watching films."

"Media tells you what to think. You believe everything you see and hear without asking yourself if it is true. You simply sit back and watch what is in front of you."

"That's not good," Maddie said, shaking her head.

"The Toxicodons have tried to make Earthlings stupid and lazy. They poisoned the food, the air and the water. They turn people against each other," replied Fraxinus sadly. "It's a good thing not all Earthlings are like this!" he said, looking directly at Maddie and James.

"How can we help?" cried James. "This is terrible!"

Fraxinus responded, "James, you already help."

"I do? How?" asked James, perplexed.

"You and your sister are healers. You heal the planet through your kind words and deeds. You are a beacon of light for people that need you. You think for yourselves. Look at the light that surrounds your bodies."

"Oh, that's just from the electric shock!" grinned James.

"Yes, you had an electric shock, James - but that only amplified the light you both carry in your hearts," laughed Commander Fraxinus. "Always carry that light with you and shine your light brightly.

In life there will always be tests. You both passed the test when neither of you would leave the other to face the Toxicodons alone."

"The white squirrel saved us from the toxic beings, can you help us find her so we can return her home?" pleaded Maddie.

"She is home. She has crossed over the rainbow bridge," replied Fraxinus.

"What do you mean?" asked Maddie, a look of concern creeping over her face.

"Don't be sad," whispered the commander. "She fulfilled her soul plan when she helped you. She has come home. She experienced all she needed from this life. She is reunited with her family members."

A silent tear rolled down Maddie's face. "Soul plan? What is that?" murmured Maddie.

"It's quite complicated to explain, but in simple terms, everyone chooses the experiences they will face on Earth before they are born." replied Fraxinus.

"I don't really understand soul plans. If they exist, I don't think they work. Nobody would choose to be ill, poor or lonely." said Maddie.

"They certainly do work... when souls choose their next life they will learn, and evolve. They know that once they have completed their plan, they will once again cross the rainbow bridge, and all will be well."

"Will we be staying here? Have we fulfilled our soul plan?" Maddie asked.

"No Maddie, your work has only just begun. You have faced numerous challenges and experienced so much in your short life. These difficulties enable you to understand others. You have 'walked in their shoes'," said Fraxinus.

Maddie looked into the commander's deep blue eyes as he continued to talk. "An exciting path is unfolding in front of you. It will lead you to help many life forms. You and your brother will lead fulfilled lives.

You were born at this time to help Planet Earth. Shine your light always. You will help to raise Earth's vibration and remove the shackles around your planet. You will assist in sending the Toxicodons back to their galaxy!"

"That would be great," laughed James. "I never want to see those toxic beings again. They have no feelings and I don't want them spreading their poison on Earth."

"You are both powerful healers. You have the most precious gift anyone can be given. I know you will use this gift wisely. Come, my officer will return you to your tree." said the commander warmly.

"Thank you, Commander Fraxinus." grinned James, excited that he would finally be going home, and thankful for the exotic fruit he had managed to squeeze into his mouth and trouser pockets.

Maddie waved goodbye to the commander with mixed feelings. She was glad to be returning to the farm, but sad that there would be one less soul climbing the Majesty Tree.

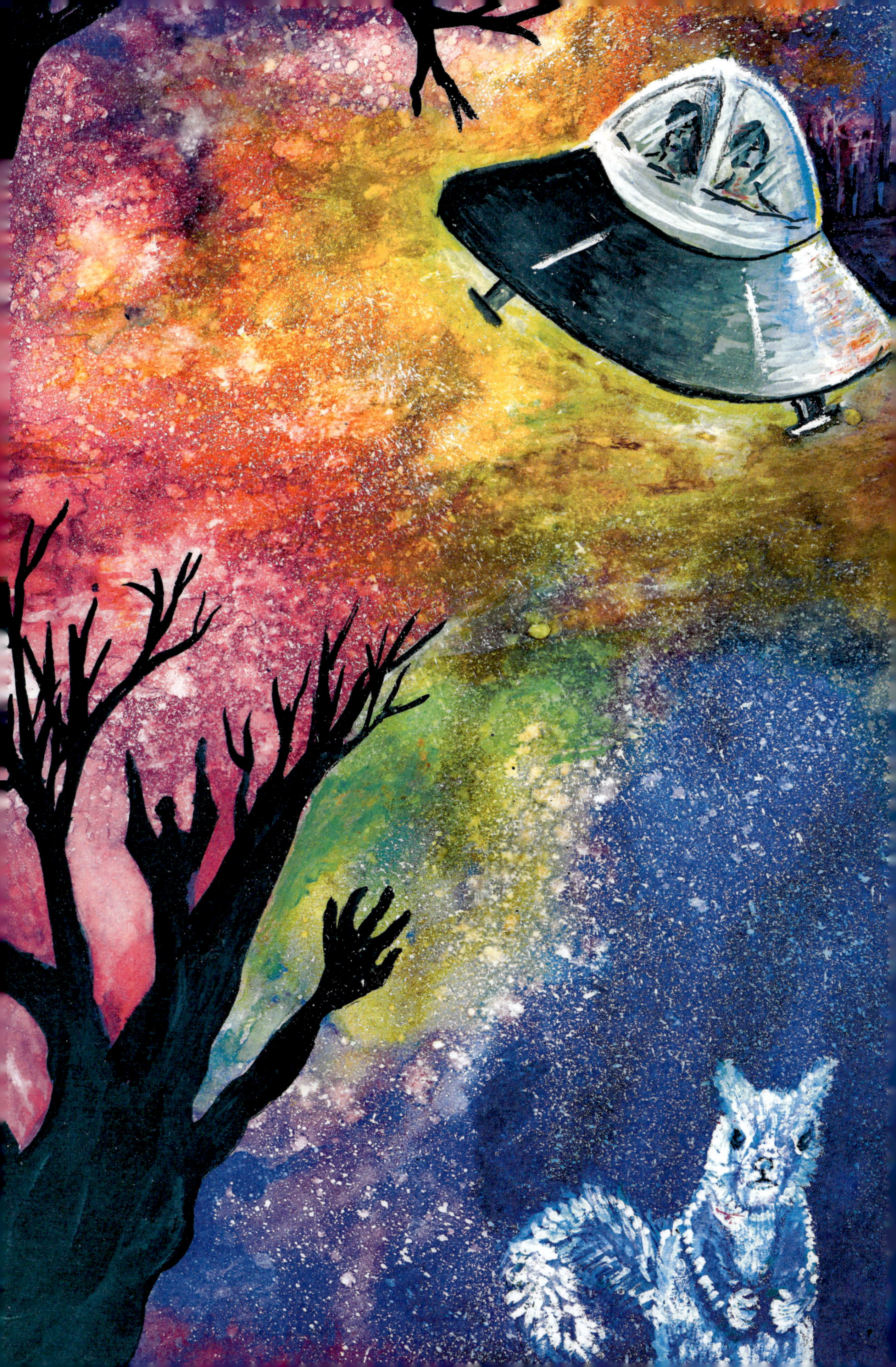

The beam ship only took a few minutes to returned Maddie and James to the Majesty Tree. Once again they found themselves at the top of the oak. The fog had dispersed and they could see clearly their farm below.

As they grabbed the branches James squealed in delight. "Look, the squirrel's drey. I knew she lived in this tree." Where two branches met, a large nest made of shredded bark, dry grass and leaves was beautifully moulded.

Maddie peeked inside. To her amazement three tiny fur babies were sound asleep. "Oh James, the squirrel sacrificed herself for us - now it is our turn to return the favour."

Maddie collected the tiny squirrels and gave them to James to snuggle under his jumper. "What's three more mouths to feed?" giggled Maddie as her feet finally touched the ground.

Hand in hand, Maddie and James walked towards the barn. They couldn't wait to tell their parents about the world beyond the Majesty Tree and introduce them to the latest family members!

***

"I have just realised something," said Darion

"What's that?" Iridiana replied with a twinkle in her eye.

"That we are given gifts every day, from the wind on our scales to the stars that light the sky at night. Small things, when added together, are the ingredients for a happy life."

"Very profound!" replied Iridiana. "In appreciating the small things in life, great abundance occurs within. A single flower in a meadow may not give off much fragrance but when accompanied by other flowers its scent will help our souls blossom."

"I am so lucky that I have you in my life." Darion whispered to Iridiana as his claws clasped his aunt's and his scales shone brightly.

"Oh Darion, it is me that is blessed to have you. Do you know what your name means?"

"No, my mother and father never told me," uttered Darion.

"It means 'Gift'! Your parents would be so proud of you. You really are the most precious gift."

Darion's face beamed. "Aunty, I think your name must mean 'Rainbow'. You bring colour to my life."

Iridiana placed her wings over Darion's shoulders. She felt as if her heart was going to burst. Her nephew was finally learning the value of his special place in life.

Bit by bit he learned to let go of the pain he had been holding. In letting go, Darion found more space in his heart to love. Iridiana knew Darion would make a fine Water Dragon. He would pass on the teachings of his dragon ancestors to those that would listen and wanted to learn.

Even in the darkness, the most difficult path can be lit by love. Beyond the night sky, the Moon, the stars, celestial worlds shine, even when obscured by clouds.

What's in a name?

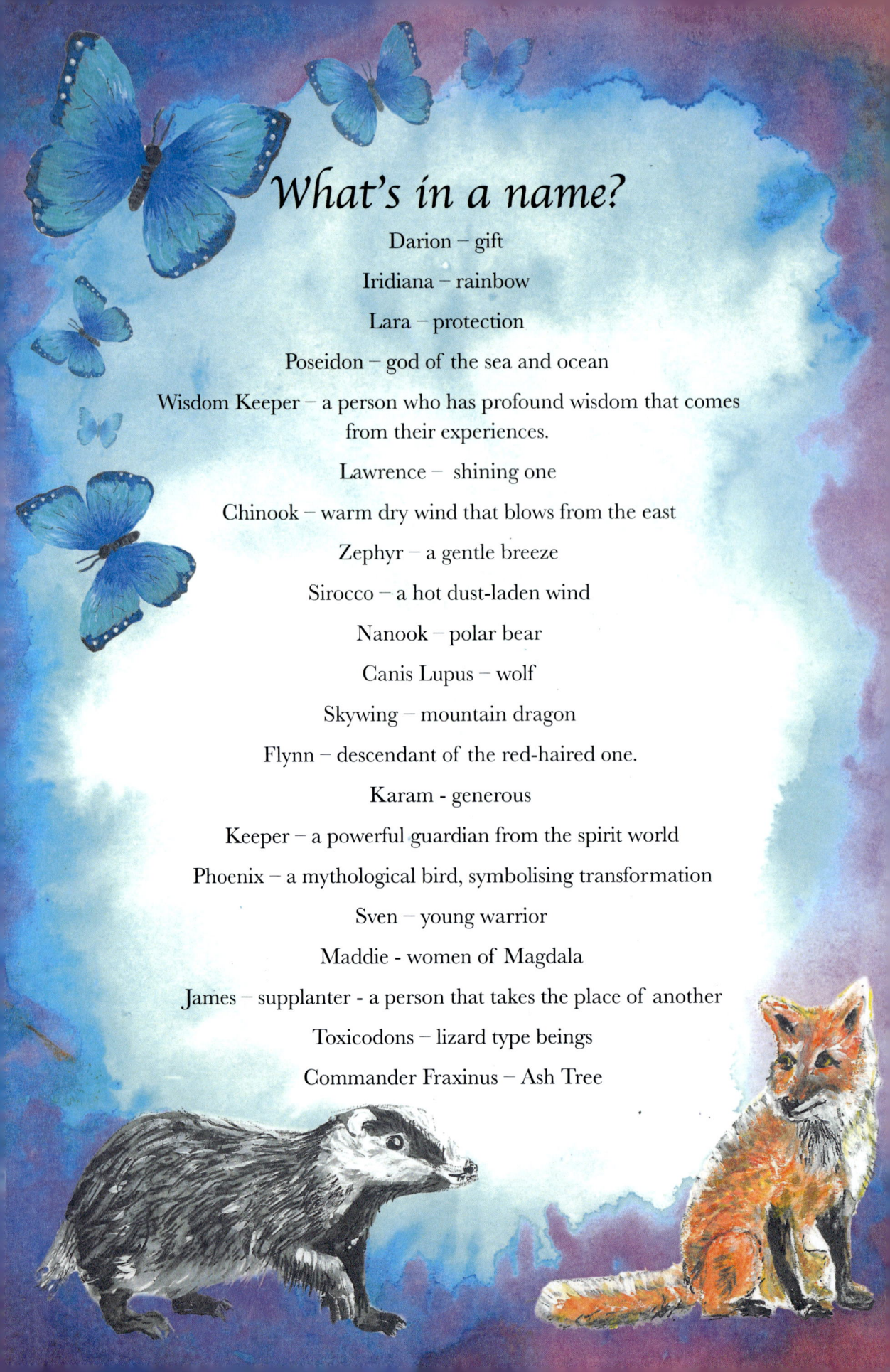

Darion – gift

Iridiana – rainbow

Lara – protection

Poseidon – god of the sea and ocean

Wisdom Keeper – a person who has profound wisdom that comes from their experiences.

Lawrence – shining one

Chinook – warm dry wind that blows from the east

Zephyr – a gentle breeze

Sirocco – a hot dust-laden wind

Nanook – polar bear

Canis Lupus – wolf

Skywing – mountain dragon

Flynn – descendant of the red-haired one.

Karam - generous

Keeper – a powerful guardian from the spirit world

Phoenix – a mythological bird, symbolising transformation

Sven – young warrior

Maddie - women of Magdala

James – supplanter - a person that takes the place of another

Toxicodons – lizard type beings

Commander Fraxinus – Ash Tree

Dragon Wisdom

Speak your truth from your heart

Let tears flow freely, for they help to release the sadness you carry

Trust your instinct. If something doesn't feel right, walk away

Know that your words are powerful, use them responsibly

Fly wingtip to wingtip with the mighty Eagles, for they look at life from a higher perspective

Stand in your power

See magic in all things

Understand you are never alone

Acknowledgements

I would like to extend my gratitude and appreciation to the following individuals and organizations for their contribution to Darion's Gift.

Christopher John Ball, a remarkable fine arts photographer, campaigner, and writer. An unsung hero, whose unwavering support breathed life into the very essence of my dream.

Dawn Smith, a wonderful companion on my journey, tirelessly proofreading my story and sharing her ideas.

Nic Whitham from Banyan Retreat, for taking the time to immerse himself in my story, providing invaluable encouragement.

Tam Winstone, whose generous contribution of her father's paints and paper awakened my creativity and inspiration.

Amanda Angus, the editor, who has poured her expertise and dedication into my work.

Mathew Woodhams, R K Graphics, Dover, for his skills in formatting the final copy. Ensuring every detail is the way it was meant to be.

Lastly, to my family and friends. I am forever grateful to each and every one of you for your belief in me and for being part of this journey. A journey where the seeds of ideas have been planted into inquiring young mines to grow and help them navigate through life's ups and downs.

I now embark upon my own journey to gain more experience before I put pen to paper once more. I still have much to write!

Printed and bound by CPI Group (UK) Ltd, Croydon, CR0 4YY
26/11/2023
03594309-0001